I0456448

LOREN

TATE'S CROSSING BOOK 4

KATHI S. BARTON

This is a work of fiction. Names, characters, places, and incidents are products of the author's imagination or are used fictitiously and are not to be construed as real. Any resemblance to actual events, locations, organizations, or persons, living or dead, is entirely coincidental.

World Castle Publishing, LLC

Pensacola, Florida
Copyright © 2023 Kathi S. Barton
Paperback ISBN: 9798891260603
eBook ISBN: 9798891260610
First Edition World Castle Publishing, LLC, September 25, 2023
http://www.worldcastlepublishing.com

Licensing Notes

Cover: Karen Fuller
Editor: Karen Fuller

Prologue

Andy had been working with the young woman for about three weeks now. She didn't say much. Hardly anything at all, as a matter of fact. But the two of them worked well together washing up the dishes after people finished up with their dinner in the restaurant. He was happy to be able to get out of the restaurant at a decent hour nightly, mostly because of her. Not only did she work really well, but she'd told him short cuts that they could use that had saved them both a great deal of time and energy. As old as he was, Andy didn't like using up his energy by doing things the wrong way.

"Twelve thousand forty-one." She did that a great deal too. When a string of numbers was said, it seemed to him about any place in the restaurant. She would total them up quicker than the person who was adding them could. Especially the boss man. Even with the boss using a calculator, she usually had them all added up and was correct about it as well.

But she said it low so that no one would hear her, he guessed. No point in getting the boss in a tizzy when there was no reason for it. Andy was sure, too, that the only reason that he'd been able to hear her was that he was a wolf. She'd been that low.

"Twelve thousand forty-two." Before he could remind himself that he needed to keep his mouth shut on certain things, he corrected the man who had been adding up the numbers. "What did you say, Andy? You thinking that you're smarter than my phone is?"

"No, sir. I didn't think that at all." He glanced over at Hanna and saw the terror on her face as she shook her head at him. "No. I was just keeping a running total in my head when you kept repeating yourself. I'm more than likely wrong."

Mr. Hendershot walked away but did return a few minutes later to tell Andy that he'd been correct in his adding. That was another thing that he liked about working here—and there weren't that many things—they were quick to tell you that you'd done a good job. Quicker, too, sometimes to tell you that you didn't, but he didn't make that many mistakes anymore just by keeping his mouth closed all the time. Best way to keep a job, he thought.

After the dinner rush, he and Hanna were allowed to have a break. There were plenty enough dishes and glasses to set up the tables again, so they were free from the hot room washing dishes for an entire thirty minutes this time. Usually, he would sit out on the steps, and Hanna would disappear someplace else. But today, she sat down next to him on the stairs. He shared his carrots and celery with her with barbeque sauce. She only took the carrots, he noticed, and not dipping them.

She didn't seem inclined to empty her head. He'd noticed that right off if she had something to say, then she'd say it. Otherwise, she'd just sit there and not say a word for hours on end. Andy supposed that was why he had taken to listening to the radio when they worked together. It staved off the too quiet of clanking dishes and tinging silverware sounds. That was a sound that he'd hear in his sleep. Clank-clank-clank.

"There are seven men in the dining room that are looking for me." Startled out of his thoughts, he asked Hanna if she needed his help. "No. I don't really need anyone's help, but I wanted you to know because they're going to come into the kitchen in a few minutes and open fire on the people there. I don't want you to be hurt. Will you do what I tell you, Andy? I really have no desire for anyone to be harmed, but especially you."

"I see." He didn't really but thought of what she was telling him. "You're not human, are you? I'm not either, in the event you might not have noticed. I'm a wolf, not at all like them kind on the television. This time of year, what with Halloween coming soon, there are lots of scary movies on."

"No. I'm not human. But I'm powerful enough to keep you safe." When she didn't say anymore, he nodded. Andy did think about what she'd said about the seven men and asked her about them. "Why are they looking for you? If you can tell me."

"I can't. However, if you value your life, which I'm assuming most people do, then when the break time is over, don't go back into the building. Once you're inside, it will be the end of your life. I can't save you if you're already dead. Do you understand that? They will not leave anyone alive in their pursuit of finding me so that there are no witnesses left behind." He said he wasn't going back in. However, he did ask about the others in the kitchen. "The chef is getting everyone out of the area as we sit here because I suggested it to him with my magic. He's been keeping tabs on the two of us so he can point right to us when the men come into the kitchen. He's not at all loyal to anyone but himself. But he won't have time to point them out to us as he's a coward and has already left the building in favor of going home before it begins. I'm glad that I was able to have him warn the others. While he knows that these men are looking for a dishwasher, he didn't bother finding out if they were looking for a male or female and sold us both out. He'll be taken care of later tonight."

A chill of fear raced up and over his spine when she said that. Andy didn't want to know what she meant by that as he was sure she meant that he was going to die. However, he also thought that the man would suffer in ways that no one before him had ever suffered before, too. Andy couldn't shake the feeling that he needed to keep close to Hanna and keep her on his good side for some reason. He might be well into his late fifties, working this job to have extras like food on his table. He liked living too much to let someone kill him for no reason.

Standing up when the little alarm he had on his phone went off, Andy made his way deeper into the parking lot, following Hanna. There were lights out all over the lot, he just noticed, and that, too, scared him a bit. He thought that would be the best place to hide for both of them. When she stopped suddenly, he did as well. His wolf, right there on the edge of his fear, seemed to understand better than he did what was coming for the two of them.

"Stay here." Dropping down to his belly, he rolled under the car when Hanna told him to take cover. He was glad that he'd been looking at her feet from his position on the ground, or he might well have scared twenty years off his life when she turned into a cat. Not a little bitty one either, but a big one that he'd seen in a zoo one time.

Sleek came to mind when she lowered her head to look at him. Her fur was so dark that it looked like the darkened sky was brighter. Her eyes were dark, too. He'd noticed that about her when she'd been just a person. Right now, they looked like the deepest part of a well that was deeper than he'd ever seen before. Andy watched as she shifted from her cat to falcon in a matter of seconds. When she flew off, he had an idea that she was going to take care of the threat from the sky. Had he been able to fly, that's what he would have done.

Closing his eyes, fearful of what else he might see, Andy knew that he was going to need some help when all this hit the papers, like getting himself a good lawyer. He just knew that people were going to blame him for the crap that was going to happen tonight. His alpha would be the first one to turn him in, too, if there was a reward. Didn't even have to be much. He'd do it for ten cents if that was what they were offering.

His own pack leader, Jerome, wasn't all that good of a leader. In fact, Andy thought that he could have done a much better job of keeping the pack together than he had been only a tiny wenny bit better at paying attention. He didn't make much of an effort to do much of anything but eat. Jerome was old, fat and lazy. And if there was any way for him to get out of doing anything at all, he'd be the first in line to not have to work.

Andy thought about other leaders that he'd met in his fifty-some years on this earth. The one that he compared all the others to was his good friend Joseph Tate. The two of them had grown up together when they'd just been pups. But when his momma and daddy had decided to go where there might be more work, he was taken to the pack he was in now. Reaching for Joseph now, thinking he needed someone in his corner for a change, he was surprised when he knew just who he was.

"*Are you all right, Andy? My goodness, it's been a long time since we've spoken. I'm thinking that it's been nearly forty years by now.*" He said that he needed his help. Then told him what was going on. "*You say this girl, she's a shifter? You thinking that's what they're after to breed her or something.*"

"*I don't know. She is super smart. That's about all I know about her. And until a few minutes ago, I didn't know she was a shifter either. She didn't smell like anything at all, now that I'm thinking on it.*" Joseph told him it was best for her to keep that under her hat. "*Yes, I can see that. I like her, and I'd hate to have her upset with me, Joesph. She's intense.*"

After telling him where he was and how he wanted to join his pack, Joseph told him how his oldest was now the pack leader and doing a darn fine job of it. Andy felt his disappointment all the way to his toes on hearing that.

"*I'm coming for you, Andy. You just sit tight. Me and a couple of my boys will be there in an hour or less. I'm bringing Joel, too. And his pretty little mate. She's scarier than anyone I've ever met before, so you keep yourself together when she talks to you. She'll take you to task if you even suggest that they shouldn't have bothered with you."* He wasn't sure what he meant by that but said he'd be on his best behavior. Just then, he heard gun shots behind him.

There were lots of them, too. Sometimes, he couldn't tell one from the other they'd been so fast. But he kept his head down, and his eyes closed. Whatever was going on, he knew that he'd be all right if he listened to Hanna. Then he remembered that his friend Joseph was coming and he didn't want him to be ambushed. His family, either.

"I think it's started in the restaurant, Joseph. She told me there'd be seven of them, but it sounds like there is a war going on behind me." The screams that he could hear all the way out in the parking lot were cut off, and he had a feeling that not everyone made it out of the place alive. As he lay there, keeping his fear at bay, he heard a scream as well as someone screaming.

Not like a painful scream but that of a large cat that was about as pissed off as he'd ever heard of. Not having any idea what was going on, he thought that staying where he was would keep him alive long enough to ask questions about what happened later. If it didn't get him into hot water with anyone. Hanna had saved him, and he'd do whatever she needed for the rest of his days.

He nearly screamed when the large black cat showed herself in front of him right in front of the car he was under. She didn't shift again but sat there staring at him while he was lying there thinking of his heart pounding so hard. Putting out her large paw, much larger than his own paw would have been, he put his hand into it and waited to see if she'd hurt him or not.

The lick to his face was so unexpected that he whimpered. It was a connection he realized as soon as she backed away from him. Usually, he'd have to take a bit of blood from a person, but apparently not his Hanna. Then she laughed a little.

"You're going to be just fine, Andy. I promise you. But I've been shot, and I need for you to call someone to come and help me. Please. I wasn't paying as much attention as I should have, and I got myself shot up pretty badly. But there are things here that need to be taken care of. Can you do that for me, please?"

He told her how he'd called his good friend Joseph Tate, and he was coming for him. When the cat lay down, he moved over so that she could get under the car with him if she wanted. Instead, she just lay there. That was when he smelled fresh blood. Also, her magic. He could taste it on his tongue.

She wasn't just stronger than him, he realized, but she was very powerful. Like one of them queens he'd read about when he'd been in school. Mother of the Earth and all the others. She was as magical as them, if not more, he thought.

"Can I remove the bullet from you?" She told him that she didn't think it would be removed with anything but magic. "As a wolf, I have me some, but I'm thinking that you're going to need a wee bit more than I have."

"*Yes. But you've no idea how much I appreciate you offering, Andy.*" He wanted to help her but wasn't entirely sure what he could do anyway. "*The people that are coming, one of them can help me if he wishes. I can feel his magic from where they are to us.*"

"I'll make him do it." The laughter coming from her was cut off when he heard the crunch of gravel not far from where they were hiding. He spoke to her through their connection so as not to draw any unwanted attention to them. "*What can I do to keep you safe? I don't want you to hurt any more than you are right now."*

"He won't see either of us. We'll be all right. None of them will ever see us for now." He didn't know why he believed her, but he did. So when the men, three of them walked right by them without saying a word, Andy knew that he had to warn Joseph of the people with guns around them. *"Tell your friend that he needs to contact the Queen of the Earth to hide any traces of me being here. She'll know what to do."*

He did just that. Andy could feel Joseph's humor with that. When he spoke, it brought a smile to his own face. It had been a long time since they'd spoken, but Andy remembered that Joseph had a crackin' good sense of humor.

"So she's got herself some connections, does she? Well, I'll have my son, Cliff, he's with me contact her. They're pretty close, I guess. You're keeping safe, aren't you, my friend? I don't want you to be hurt, either." Andy told his good friend that Hanna, the woman, was watching out for him. *"Good for the both of you. You just wait on us, Andy, and we'll be there in two shakes of a lamb's tail."*

While he hadn't any idea what that meant about his son Cliff and the lady queen being close, he was in too deep right now to question much of anything. Terror, like he was feeling right now, had his brain all scrabbled up too much to think straight, much less ask important questions.

Andy felt the earth move under his body and reached out to pull Hanna, as her cat, closer to him. The need to protect her was overwhelming. He'd not felt a need like this since his own wife had been around. When the lady of the earth and faeries appeared, he felt himself being lifted up and carried away. Like the car that he'd been under hadn't been there at all.

He didn't know where he was going, nor did he care right now. They were going to be safe, and he was happier than he'd been in a while to know that. As he was being laid down, a small creature landed near his hand. Lifting his hand up to see the little person, she smiled at him.

"I'm to tell you that the queen has made sure that your pack leader isn't going to come after you for anything that happened at the restaurant. She said that you were as safe as you'd be if she was here with you. Also, she wanted me to inform you, Master Andy, that the young lady that you were with is in good hands, and her wounds are healing nicely. The queen will thank you herself for making sure not much more harm came to her." He thanked her for that. "You are most welcome. I don't need to tell you that you're in a magical realm, sir. No one will bother you, nor will you be taken to task by anyone here. This room is yours to roam around as much as you wish. There is a garden beyond those doors there that you are welcome to visit as well. Do you need anything from me?"

"No. Wait, yes. Joseph and his sons, are they all right too?" She said that they were doing very well and have been well compensated for helping him and the lady Hanna. "She's special to the queen, I think. I don't know why, but I have a feeling that she's very special to a great many people."

"She is at that, sir. Very special to all of us." When he couldn't think of anything else, he felt himself sliding into deep sleep. The little person spoke once again, dragging him up from his need to sleep once more. "You must rest. Once you are well rested and well, everything will be explained to you. But for now, my lord, you must make sure that you are able to regain your strength."

He didn't want to sleep but wanted to ask what she'd meant. But sleep was beckoning him, and he couldn't fight it any longer. Letting his mind clear of all the things that had happened, Andy knew on some level that this wasn't going to be a simple case of him helping a shifter out when she needed it. There was something stronger and bigger than he'd been involved in before.

Honestly, he couldn't wait to see Hanna again. He'd liked her, and the fact that she'd thought enough of him to save him tonight made him feel very protective of the…woman. He no more thought that she was younger than him than he did he was going to be an Alpha.

~*~

Loren was walking around the greenhouse today. He was bored and had thought that getting out of his house and head would be good. Then he spotted a couple of faeries in the front office. Thinking that was strange, he made his way through the hot rooms to where he could see them.

Coming here to the green house, thinking that he'd really like some help on planting a few things around his house, he was surprised to find Aurora sitting at the desk where the little people were. She smiled at him as he took a seat. Jasmine, one of the many faeries that he'd met over the last few days, sat on his knee.

"'Tis almost winter." He told her that it was still a few months away, but he loved the crispness of the air. "Soon enough, it will be too cold to plant anything, and you need to get your house in order, Mr. Loren. You've been remiss in—"

"Jasmine." She turned to look at Aurora when she spoke. "Mr. Loren is well aware of the lateness of the year. He is in here wishing to find things to plant. Are you not, Loren?"

There was a twinkle in her eyes, and he smiled after saying that was just what he was here for. But he did tell Jasmine that he also needed help. Loren told the little being that he didn't know much about flowers and plants and wondered if she could help him. The way her wings fluttered, he thought she might well be more excited to help him than he was to get started.

"You need plenty of roses. Of all colors. We'll care for those for you. At one time, the home that you live in now was a showcase of flowers and blooms. All of them were so bright and happy. Many a night, I would go to the yard where you are living and watch as the moon light brightened the dew there and made them shine." He told her that his mother had loved roses. "Yes, I remember that about her, too. It was such a pleasure to go to her gardens and make sure she had the most beautiful blooms. We so loved it when she would pick some of the blooms and take them into her home. Your mother was a good woman, Mr. Loren. A great person who took care of us by leaving us small treats and letting us care for the flowers there."

"She knew there were faeries? I mean, I heard of your kind, but I guess it never occurred to me that you were real. I'm happy that you are, don't get me wrong." He closed his mouth, knowing on some level that he wasn't making any sense to even himself. "I wish to thank you for making my mother happy with her flowers. When I was just a child, she would take me to her gardens and tell me all the names of the flowers there and how they could be used for other things like teas and cookies. I remember nights, too, when the entire house would smell of her freshly cut blooms. Not just roses but the daisies that she grew in different areas around the house. The lilacs and canna lilies, too, were among my favorites. They would grace our table nightly while they were in bloom. I remember the small vases of all sorts of flowers gracing even the darkest part of the house. They would brighten that area so that you'd want to sit there. Thank you so much for those memories."

"That was the nicest story, Mr. Loren. I thank you for it. I shall tell the others how it made you feel if you would allow it." He said that he'd be grateful for her to also tell the others how happy they made them all, too. "I shall. I shall, indeed. Your mother was a great woman to all of the creatures about. Her cooking skills weren't the best, but she could take a seed and make it into so much more than a bloom or two."

After Jasmine said she'd take care that he had what was needed in his gardens, he stayed and spoke to Aurora. He had been surprised to find her in the greenhouse when he knew for a fact that she had much larger and even better-equipped ones in her own realm. Asking her about it, the smile she gave him made him think that he was in for a rare treat from her.

"The lovely young lady that is working here, Shari, she has asked that some of the faeries come and work with her—behind the scenes, so to speak. She wishes to also expand the building in favor of having other items that she believes will sell. Herbs, for one thing, and trees. Trees for my little ones are a good source of not just the fruit that some will bear but also a place for them to build their homes. She is a natural at running this place for your brother. And her taking to my little ones that came to see her was like she'd seen them all her life." He said that he'd heard that he'd given it to her to run. "She said as much to me, too, when she asked to speak to me. She has a brilliant mind, too. I think she hides it well until she is in need of it. Much like you do at times."

"I've not had much opportunity to spend any time with any of the new family members. I've been working on things around my home when I'm not working for the family. What else did you want from me, Aurora? I know as well as you do that this isn't a social visit. You have something to say, so please say it." She smiled at him. Unlike the other smiles she's been giving him today, this one was slightly sad. Right then, he wasn't sure that he wanted to know but also knew that he'd need the information from her as well. "Tell me."

"The woman, Hanna. The woman that your family went to help last evening. She is your mate. Things are progressing to the point where it must happen sooner rather than later. It's her father, you see." He didn't bother telling her that he'd been around her and she wasn't. The queen knew a great deal more about things than he ever would. "I have, for her safety and somewhat yours, kept her scent hidden away from everyone that would seek to find her. The men at the restaurant, as I'm sure the family will find out, were part of a group that her father had hired to kill her. I don't know why he thought that she'd die from anything put to her, but he's not really all that smart. He never has been. Burton is a greedy bastard who doesn't care what he does to get all that he wants. And it's her magic that he craves more than anything."

"I gather that now that you've told me, I'll feel it." She said not yet. Her scent with his would draw too much attention from her father. "Will she be stronger with me claiming her? Not that I'd do that without her permission or knowledge, but I also don't want to get her hurt either."

"I have a story to tell you." As soon as the door opened and Hanna came in, she sat down on a chair that hadn't been there before. When she glared at him, he couldn't help it. Loren laughed. She was adorable to him. Even before he'd been told she was his mate. "I was just about to tell your mate here the story of your birth."

"It's what drove my father over the edge.

Although, if you ask me, I think he was nuts before we were born." Loren asked her what she meant by her saying *we*. "I was the first born of triplets. All girls and born within seven minutes of each other. That's important, the seven minutes. It holds magical powers for our kind. Not the minutes so much as the number seven. Anyway, my mother died before we were born. I have no proof of it, but I believe that he had a hand in her death. Only by the magic that the healers gave her while we were being born of her is the only thing that saved us. Or me. Once I was born, I received a great deal of magic. Being the firstborn, it was rightfully mine to take. When my sister was born after me, she too received magic, but not nearly as much as I had. Then, the third child came. She was tiny, much smaller than either myself or my sister and died too soon to receive her magic. She had no name, but it's doubtful that she would have lived long enough to have been titled with anything had Burton not killed her."

"But she died too, the second child." Nodding, they both looked at Aurora. "Please tell me that you didn't have anything to do with them dying. I'll never forgive you if — "

"I didn't know anything about their birth, or I

would have saved the three of them. I don't like that you jumped to that conclusion, but I will forgive you this one time. When Shannon, Hanna's mother, was murdered, I, along with all the magical creatures, we were grief-stricken by it. It was felt throughout the worlds, both this one here and my own. I had been told that she hadn't bore her children before her death, and like all creatures, we assumed the worse. By the time I felt Hanna being given her magic and her father declaring her his successor, it was too late for the other two. He had murdered them himself so that—he thought so, at least, he'd be able to make Hanna do what he wanted. I've no idea what his thinking might have been on that, but then, as I've said, Burton is a fool." He asked how the second child died. Aurora looked at Hanna before answering him. "Burton murdered her, as I said. He took a blade and removed her head with it. The same with the other child. As it was, he'd killed his own wife when he thought that she was going behind his back and undoing his punishments to his subjects. She *was* doing that. It was why the people were so grief-stricken by her death. She was well and truly loved by every creature that ever met her. Subjects, it's what he called the shifters. He was there to keep safe but punished harshly to the point of near death. After I found out that Shannon had died by his hand, too, I did some digging, and all I could find was that he was the last person to see her before her death. I have nothing to prove he'd done it. It's been centuries, Loren and I'm no closer to finding what he did than I was all those years ago. He needs to be taken to task, killed, I mean, for what he's done."

"Is that all? I mean, he's only going to be killed? I would like to see him punished, suffering badly for killing his own child. I'm sure that Hanna would as well. Not to mention trying to kill Hanna. Please tell me that was just a rumor that you've heard. What sort of monster does something like that to his own flesh and blood? Not to mention the mother of his own children. Christ, I'm going to find out what I can as well." He looked at Hanna. "I'm so very sorry for your losses, Hanna. It wounds me deep in my heart that you've had to deal with such a monster. I'll do everything in my power to keep you safe."

"He'll harm you in ways that you'll wish for death when he finds out that you are my mate. And it's only a matter of time before he does." He said that so long as she was safe, he didn't care. "You mean that, don't you? You'd lay down your life for someone that you barely know."

"I would. Without a second thought to anything but you." He took her hand into his and could feel the buzz of magic that she was sharing with him. "You're my mate, Hanna. I wish that I could declare it, but it's safer for me to hold onto that for a time. You are my life now, and I will do anything to keep you safe for all time."

"He'll come for me soon. It won't matter to him what you are or what kind of relationship that we have." He asked her what he could do to make it so that he was strong enough to take him on. "I need to change you into what I am. That will only happen if you declare that I'm your mate, and I do the same. You'll be king, someone that he cannot touch because you'll no longer be only a simple shifter but a magical one. Stronger than even the queen here. You and I together will be able to end the world should we wish it. Not that I do that, but I'm just trying to make you aware of how much power the two of us will have."

"I declare that you, Hanna—I don't know your last name." She told him that she'd never had one. But she did use Jones when she had to. "Then I declare you, Hanna Jones Tate, to be my mate."

They were still holding hands when he finished his simple declaration. When Hanna repeated the words back to him, telling him that she took him as her mate, a sort of calm rolled over him, and he could feel his wolf being changed as he sat there. When she smiled at him, he could have taken on the world and come out on top because he suddenly realized that he was in love with his pretty mate.

The two of them sat in the office and talked about things that she'd been able to find out about her father. They held hands the entire time. It was calming to him, and he thought to her as well. It was a good deal more information than he thought anyone had. Then they spoke about her castle in the realm that Aurora was in.

"Do you go there often?" Hanna told him that she'd not been there for a while as she was sure that was where her father was hiding out close to it so that he could pounce on her. "I'm assuming that, unlike this realm, there isn't any way to track him through the earth."

"You'd be correct. So long as he stays within the property surrounding the castle, no one will be able to pinpoint his exact location. But he can't enter the castle or any of the other buildings without my permission. That would be you as well. Since you are king to my queen, you have as much power as I do when it comes to making decisions. Once he was declared unfit by the royals of other realms to be king, I was next in line and received all that he was. But for a little magic to keep him healthy, he has nothing to keep him from being killed. He has other perks, too. Mostly ones that are what is getting him in trouble. Like he's built him a house with his magic. It had taken him days before he was able to wake from the loss of that much magic. That is how weak he is now." He asked her if there was a jury or something like that to take him to task. "Not while he's in the castle proper. I can go there and do it, and I'm better equipped now that we're mates to do it. But I know this is nuts, but he's my father. And even though he's killed everything around him, including the ones that he should have loved, it's difficult for me to even contemplate killing him by magic. If I were destroyed, which you and your brother Cliff with his mate can do, he will also be destroyed. That is the only way that I can think to make it so he doesn't harm anyone else. Especially all shifters."

"I'm not going to do that. Not ever." She told him that it might well be the only way to save all the shifters. "You said it *might* be the only way. I will work on finding that other way. If Cliff and Shade can help me, I'll get their help as well. Between the four of us, we'll take care of the man. I swear to you on my mother's heart that you'll not have to worry about him again."

He had no idea how he was going to do it. Loren didn't understand a lot of what was going on. But she was his mate, his only love, and he was going to make sure that no harm came to her, by her hand or her father's.

Reaching out to his family, he let them know that he had found his mate and that it was Hanna. They were happy for them both, and Joel asked if the two of them would join them for dinner tonight. After asking Hanna, he told them that they'd be there and that he needed to tell them a few things, too. Asking Cliff if he could talk to him soon, his brother told him that he was at home now if the two of them wanted to come by.

"By the way, we felt your declaration of taking Hanna as your mate. It nearly knocked me on my ass. I'm so happy for you, Loren." He said that he was, too. *"Come over soon. We're going to dinner too at Joel's."*

Since he'd driven over to the green house, he

and Hanna drove to his home first so that she could figure out if she liked it well enough to live there or not. Teasing him, something no one had ever done before, she told him she'd been living in a box until recently. A small hut would have been better than that.

Cliff hugged them both and told them how happy he was for them. Once they were settled in the large living room, the three of them talked about the upcoming auction that would sell off a large estate of goods. Shade joined them just as he was beginning to tell Cliff what was going on and how he needed his help.

~*~

Burton wasn't happy with the hut he was living in. It wasn't really a hut, but with the castle that he'd been banned from, the place he had now was all he would call it. Two bedrooms, a kitchen and some kind of gathering room were all he had besides a bathroom.

"Damned girl. Where does she get off thinking that she can treat me like this? I'm her father, for fuck sake." He wasn't even sure about that either. That's why he'd killed her mother. "She shouldn't have birthed them babies at all, damn it. They're not mine."

He knew that to be a lie. Handle, or whatever her name was, looked just like him when she'd been nothing but a weak-assed babe. He supposed she'd not been weak either. Since she'd been able to stop his attempts of killing her, too.

Three babes. It should have been a time of celebration. Of having a grand party like he always loved. But he had been told that he needed to declare the babe as his successor. That was another lie that they'd done to him. Once he declared her as his child and his successor, everyone was out to get him, it seemed. Especially his daughter. The one that he wasn't able to kill.

The team of rulers, kings and queens of other areas around the earthly realm had been around as long as he had, told him just before his wife had given birth that he wasn't fit to be king any longer. No one knew that he'd killed his family when his child had been born. They thought it was a curse that had been laid upon him. Burton didn't want to be taken down now that all his burdens had been taken care of — his wife and two of his children. Now, all he was left with was two more. And he'd get them soon enough, Burton thought with a smile.

Handle needed to be killed. He couldn't do it,

of course. One of those laws that he had to live by. Killing his wife had been easier than he'd thought. Just letting her fall off the castle wall and be impaled on the rocky bottoms had done that for him. He didn't even have to push her; the wind had taken up then, and when she reached for him to keep her steady, he just didn't offer her his hand and had backed away so she'd not reach him. He'd never been so happy about an accident in his life.

The babes were easier to kill off. The smallest one needed magic, and he forbade it. They had to listen to him when he said that she'd be a burden to the household the way she had been affected by the fall. The second child, too. She'd been born with a broken arm and leg. It too would have been a burden, he told them, even though hers would heal.

Killing the woman who said she'd be able to set the bones so that there would be no harm done to the child was no trouble at all for him to kill. Once she was laying on the floor, her head nearly cut from her shoulder, the other agreed with everything that he said, except for the first born.

The other person that needed to be ended was his counselor. He had stolen Handle away before he could get to her. Burton knew she'd been somewhere in the castle all her life, but there was enough magic around that he could never enter some of the rooms. And since he never knew the name of his counselor, he wasn't able to summon him to bring the child. Dirty players, all of them out to get him.

So here he was, locked from the castle that should have been rightfully his and his magic was nearly depleted. Who would have thought that he'd be reduced to one such as he was now because he had a child to take over for him.

"I would have ruled forever had they kept their noses out of my business. I was a good king." Another lie, but this one made him laugh. "You bastards, just wait and see what kind of king I am when I find that child."

"Sire?" He turned to look at the man who had been seeing to his needs. He hadn't any idea what his name was either. Burton had never learned a person's name unless he had to. "All the faeries have left the grounds. They left sometime in the night. There isn't any of them in your house either, as they left as well."

"Where do they think they're going to go when I told them to stay here?" He told him that they'd returned to their own realm. "No doubt coming up with lies to tell that queen of theirs. I do hate liars, don't you?"

"Yes, sire." When the man left, Burton sat in his chair. While he knew that faeries were important to the wellbeing of the land he was on, he also knew that they could be pesky when they were annoyed. Right now, all he could think about was how quiet it suddenly was without them around.

When he decided he was hungry, he went to the kitchen area. He didn't know his way around it any more than he did the gardens that had been behind the castle all his life. Now, it was nothing more than high weeds and half-rotted tubers. Christ, he hated that he'd been reduced to that too.

He'd been required, only because his belly was forever empty, to be a gardener. He had to curry his horse, too, as there was no one to do it for him. Looking down at his boots, filthy and full of holes, Burton decided right then that he was never going to wear anything more than one time. Every piece of clothing, boots and hats would be made and laid out for him daily. It was a good decision he made, and by god, they were going to do it for him when he got his magic back from his daughter.

Entering the kitchen, he realized that there was

no one around to make him a meal. The man that was with him didn't know how to cook either. There were pots and pans, even a few gadgets that he couldn't have named if he was being held at gunpoint. But nothing for him to easily eat and fill the void of his stomach.

He found a can of something called *oysters* and poured them into a bowl. There were more than likely cooking instructions on the side of the can, but since he couldn't read nor write, it might as well have been gibberish. While it didn't look all that appetizing, he was hungry and put a large spoonful of it in his mouth.

He couldn't get them out of his mouth quick enough. They were slimy and slick. Like he was eating worms. Turning his head, he puked up everything that he'd stupidly put into his mouth, as well as bile from the bottom of his gullet. He did that five more times before he felt that he'd gotten all of it out of his body. Still, there was the lingering thought that one of them had made its way to his stomach and making itself a home there.

Staggering to the gathering room, he fell more than sat in his chair. He knew that he must look a sight, but he was too weak to do much more about it than to try and plaster his hair down so that he looked at least a little presentable. He doubted that even taking a bath, something that he abhorred more than anything, would make him look better at this moment.

Burton must have dozed off at some point. The air was putrid with the puke from the kitchen was what had awakened him. Standing up after bellowing for help, he kicked the chair around. One of the legs off it came back and hit him in the head. Falling back, he hit his head hard enough that he actually saw stars floating around his head.

Having to sit there with his head spinning, he could smell the puke again. Before he was able to stand, he got a good whiff of his clothing. Christ, oh mighty, he smelled like a wet dead horse. Nearly sick again with that odor, he decided that he was going to have to get himself some clothing if this was going to be happening. Smelling himself like this made him wonder if he could get a tailor to come to him.

For nearly two hours, he searched for someone to come to his aid. Using a little magic to clean up the mess in the kitchen still made him ill when he had to look at the things again. Why would anyone want to can something up like that was beyond him.

It looked like something that he would have blown out of his nose sometimes.

Still, no one around to help him, Burton made his way to the gardens. He knew that he'd forbade the faeries from bringing anything they grew into his home to eat, but surely they'd kept busy but doing something to the garden. He'd had no luck at all in making heads or tails of the place. What was a weed and what was a plant had tripped him up a great deal.

Burton remembered his wife bringing in some tomatoes to eat when she'd been around. He loved those little suckers with a lot of salt on them, and he'd just pop them into his mouth like they were candy bits. They sort of tasted like that, too. Sweetest little things that he'd ever tasted that wasn't cake or cookies.

The garden was devoid of anything but a couple of pumpkins. He knew that you could make some kind of pie out of them, but he wasn't going to be able to do that. While he was trying to think of anything else he could do with the fat suckers, the ground beneath his feet shook hard enough to toss him around a little.

Without looking up, he knew who had come to

see him. Aurora was another person that he wanted to kill. Of course, he couldn't do that. To kill her would be the same as killing himself. He did have plans for her, however.

"Burton, what are you going to do with that half-rotten pumpkin?" He said he was hungry and didn't appreciate her just dropping by uninvited. "You have no say where I go and who invites me. I thought that I made that clear when you begged me to come here and take the spell from the castle. You'll be thrilled to know that I have spoken to your daughter. I know that I'm happy that she is the opposite of you in all things. And she looked so much like her mother that you murdered that it hurts me at times."

"You tell her to get her ass here." Aurora threw back her head and laughed. Even though it was a lovely sound, like one would think twinkling stars would sound but he was too irritated to want to compliment her on it. "Why do you find that funny? She's my daughter, and I want her here to let me in my home."

"It is no longer your home, Burton. It hasn't been since she took her first breath. Even had you not acknowledged her as your successor, anyone with an ounce of sense could tell by being around her that she was destined to rule even you. Magic, even some that she didn't get from you, glows around her. Also, she has a mate too. Can you imagine how strong that will make her, too?" He said that he'd not given anyone permission to have a mate. "I didn't know that you were in charge of such things. I know that you're not, but to hear you tell it, you think you're able to rule myself as well. And we both know that's not true, don't we? Or would you like for me to show you once again how much you're not in charge of such things as my kingdom?"

He didn't answer her. His body had begun to ache with the remembrance of her making her point. It had been years before he'd been able to speak correctly, and even longer for his body to get back into shape so that he could walk. Christ. And all she'd done was point her finger at him and tell him to learn.

The only thing that he'd learned from her lesson was that she was a real bitch when she needed to be. And not the pushover he'd always thought her to be. Even his wife knew that. Telling him daily before she finally died that Aurora would be the end of him if he wasn't careful.

His wife had always been spouting things like that off to him. You need to do this. That needs to be worked on. Even when he was in his office, working on trying to figure out a way for him to get more magic, she would come into his office and berate him for not bathing properly. Why did a man have to bathe every day? He recked, and she told him of body odor and animal dung.

Burton had no idea where she thought he would have gotten animal dung on him. He never left the castle for anything unless it was to pick up the taxes that were owed to him. Even then, he was careful not to get too close to the people that he was supposed to be caring for.

He thought it would be obvious to anyone who knew him that he didn't care for people. Not animals, either. Burton didn't like to bathe; he thought banning it should have been a bylaw, but no one would vote with him on that. He simply wanted to be waited on, cared for, even pampered and left alone.

As for him being king, he wasn't any good at that either. Not that he gave a shit. But his lady wife did all the work. Of course, he'd take credit for it. Burton looked up at Aurora when he realized that she was still here.

"What do you have to say for yourself, Burton? Nothing good, I'm sure." He told her again to have Handle brought here. "Handle? You don't even know the name of your own child. Well, I'm not going to tell you it either. My goodness, Burton, you really are about to get your comeuppance. Soon, too."

When she disappeared, her laughter hanging around far too long after she was gone, he got up and took the pumpkin to the house. Not having any idea what to do with it, he decided that he'd have to use magic to make himself something of the orange ball.

"I'm going to make her pay for all this." The pumpkin was rotten, and he'd gotten sick again. But instead of puking in the house, Burton managed to make it to the door and out into the yard. "You little fucker, I'm going to find you, and then I'm going to kill you. Do you hear me, Handle? I'm going to make you regret ever being born."

Too sick to do much more than rest, he made his way to his bed. It, too, smelled, but he was just too exhausted to care for now. However, after lying there for ten minutes, he couldn't stand the smell anymore. He just knew that his daughter had made it so that his smeller was getting stronger. Fucker. He was going to enjoy making her pay.

Chapter 1

Hanna sat very still. Watching the men, seven of them again, wander around the town was funny to her. She didn't have any idea how they'd found her so quickly until she'd spoken to Aurora. Apparently, there were seven men in every state of this country looking for her.

"He's working his magic, what little he has left with keeping to the Seven of Magical spells. I do wonder, at times, if he can even count to seven. How do you suppose he was able to find out that significance of that?" Hanna had told Aurora that he couldn't spell much less count but that there were sevens all over the castle. "I would imagine that seeing it daily and hearing your mother talk of it would have made him remember at least that little bit. How is the number displayed there, if I may ask."

"It's not. But there are seven of nearly

everything of importance there. Seven tapestries down a single hallway. Seven chairs on either side of the long table. Seven candles in the windows during the solstices." Hanna had to laugh before continuing. "There are even seven rows planted in every garden when planting season comes around. Seven of corn, beans and other vegetables."

"I know that it has importance to you as well." She nodded and told Aurora what it meant to her. "So you're the seventh daughter born to Burton and your mother. I did not know that. It is what makes you strong, then."

"So I've been told." Now, here she sat in the little park in the center of town, watching seven men—never any women—asking if there was a stranger in town. When a shadow fell over her, she turned to look at Loren. He was forever with her but never bothered her. She found that she liked his company too. He wasn't a chatter box when quiet time was better.

"I've found some information about your father." Loren handed her a thick file, and she put it beside her on the bench. Asking him to tell her, he nodded but didn't speak. He watched the men with her. "The towns people are very loyal to us. They'll never tell them anything about you."

"I've noticed that. When asked if there are strangers in town, most of the people refer back to them. They're all strangers to the town, too." She turned to look at him. "What did you find out?"

"He's sick. Not enough to die from anything, mores the pity but sick in that he's not had a proper meal in decades, and the faeries have left him. I spoke to one of them. She told me that he stank so badly that plants would not bloom well from the stench of him. He must be pretty bad to have flowers refuse to open because of it." She laughed. It was becoming easier to find humor in things than it had been before. "Also, the man that he took with him when he was kicked out of the castle has left as well. I've yet to find a reason for that, but as of yesterday, Burton is on his own."

"Good. Without depleting his magic completely, he can't summon anyone to him either. But in order to do that, he'd have to know their names. He doesn't even know mine, so I'm not worried about him having anyone helping him." The men who were looking for her stopped in the middle of the street and stared at her. After having them believe that they'd already asked her about a stranger, they moved on. "I should have taken care of him before now, but it was just easier to let him stay where he was and not have to confront him. Now, with you around, it's important to me, to us, I guess, that he understands that he's been usurped and that he should either just leave me alone — which I don't think that he will or be killed. I've been hearing all the things, too, that he did while king. It's a small wonder that mother didn't kill him on their wedding night."

"Were they mates? The reason that I ask is that we can't harm our mates, much less kill them." Hanna explained it to him. "So how are we mates then if your kind doesn't mate for life? I mean, I know that I belong to you now, but I don't understand how it works on your kind, I guess."

"You're the same as me now, Loren. But that has nothing to do with my parents. Mother, who would have held all the magic before wedding my father needed to produce and heir. It mattered little if it was a male or female to her. The child, I mean. So long as the child would learn at her side and know the difference between right and wrong. I think that my father was…I guess you can say the pick of the realm at that time. The rules that have since been changed made it so that she could only breed with her own kind. Our kind. Also, I think that he was a fool and foolish, and my mother knew it too. He'd be easily hoodwinked about…well, about certain things that had to do with the magic. Burton never received what he'd been entitled to when he married and bonded with my mother. He had power and a bit of magic, but not nearly as much as I've shared with you. Less than a tenth of a percent, as a matter of fact. However, you're an equal to me in all things. I don't even know that it's what has him wanting me to come to him, thinking no doubt that I will do as he says as my sire. I think it was the pampered life that he is wishing to have returned to him. Someone cleaning up after him. Cooking for him. That's mostly what he complains about when he tells people that I have done him wrong."

"So you think that your father would kill you if he could simply have a life without much effort made on his part. That's the saddest thing I think I've ever heard." She agreed with him. "And this is me asking you because I don't understand him. Why not give him what he wants?" He paused in thinking, and she knew that he got it without her telling him. "Because it would never be enough. He'd always and forever want more and more from you."

"Yes." They sat there for several more minutes until she stood up. "I'm hungry. I don't usually get hungry all that often, but I'd love to share a meal with just you. While with your family last night was nice, they're too much for me right now." Loren stood up with her, and she had to look up at him.

It wasn't often that she had to do that, look up to look into a man's eyes. Hanna was just over six and a half feet tall. Loren must have been at least six inches taller than she was. It was nice, she thought, to have someone you could hold that you didn't feel like you were going to break. Then he did something so extraordinary that she almost missed what he'd said to her. He kissed her.

It was nothing more than a peck to her mouth. A quick—very satisfying kiss to her mouth like something that he'd done every day of their lives together. But she felt a surge of power from it, and she grabbed him to stand upright. He must have felt it, too, because as he held her in his arms, he swayed a bit as well.

They neither said anything for several moments. When he lifted her chin up and looked at her, she could have sworn that he had a twinkle in his eye that sent her heart into overtime. And when he spoke, his voice nothing more than a soft, sexy whisper, Hanna wanted to lean in and taste the words coming from his mouth.

"I have a feeling that when we come together sexually, it will actually be something that moves heaven and earth. Perhaps the entire solar system and beyond." Hanna continued to stare at him, watching his mouth form words and spill out. "Hanna, I know that I've only just met you a few days ago, but I want you with a passion that I've never had for anything else. That would include food as well."

"I feel the same way." She backed away from him, barely making it to the wall behind her before her knees simply gave out. "But if we give into this feeling that we're having now, it will bring every person in the world to us. If it hasn't already." Loren looked around briefly, then back at her before nodding. "Loren?"

"There are currently five of the seven men staring at us right now. I think they felt the same thing that we might have." She nodded, then looked herself at the now seven of them. "We've confused them a great deal. I think that they're only just realizing the amount of power that they're up against. Together, we do have a great deal of power, correct?"

"Yes." Putting out her hand, palm up toward the men, she watched Loren as she dealt with them. As soon as she felt them gone, Hanna looked behind her. "I've never been able to do that before. I've never been able to destroy them without using a great deal of my own power to do so."

Loren didn't say anything to her but looked where the men had been. Coming to some kind of decision, he took her hand into his, and he gently pulled her along with him. As soon as they were near one of the buildings that she'd been told was a Tate building, he opened the door and took them both inside. Pressing her against the wall, Loren told her not to move. After nodding, he left her there to exit the building again.

Hanna wanted to move. To take a look as to what he might have been doing outside without her. But he'd told her to stay put, and as much as she wanted to leave here too, for some reason, she believed that what he was doing was in their best interest. Hanna stayed where he'd told her to. When he returned, she looked at him before asking what had happened.

"Your father is here." She asked him how he knew that when she'd not felt him nearby. "I don't know. I didn't even know what he looked like before I just saw him. But he's out there. Asking after not just his men but you as well. I hope you don't mind, but I had Aurora fix it so that now that he was off the property of your — our home, the magic that allowed him to stay there was taken away."

"Thank you." Taking her hand again, he asked her what she wanted to do. "Go to the castle. With him here, I can easily go there and not be harmed by him."

Suddenly, they were in the castle proper. Not the stone castle itself but the front gates. Turning in the direction in which her father had been staying all this time, Hanna noticed that not only was the area free of his home, but all traces of him were now gone. She asked Loren what else he'd done.

"I didn't know that I could contact the earth, but they've repaired the earth with their own magic so that the harm that he did to the area has been healed. Also, you might find this hard to believe — or perhaps not — Burton will no longer be able to do anything to the earth, anywhere in either realm, unless you give him permission to do so. I don't believe that you will, but he's pretty much banded from harming even a blade of grass from now on." She asked him how he'd figured out that he could do that. "I have no idea. When I realized that he was no longer squatting on your — our land, it occurred to me that we could keep him from getting close to the castle again. So, while I was thinking about that, the information was just there. Like I knew it all along and had to have a reason for it to come to me." He looked confused for a moment before speaking again. "That doesn't make the least bit sense, does it?"

"It does. I understand. That's what happens to me when I have to...just this morning, I had a thought that one of the faeries needed some help. I know a little about faeries but not enough to know how to help them build a house that will sustain them. After one conversation with Yodel, I was able to not just help him get his house high into the tree but give him the materials that he needed to make it safeguarded against the larger creatures that are always looking for a tasty treat." He smiled at her, and she felt...well, giddy about it. "I want to do more things like that. I've been on the go, hiding from the men that my father has sent to me that I never took the time to just have a bit of fun."

"I love that idea. Come on." He nearly dragged her out of the castle and to the back of it. Once there, he put his fingers into his mouth and let out a shrill whistle that impressed her greatly. Looking where he was looking, she saw that hundreds of faeries and brownies alike came to them. "We're here to help you with any projects that you have going on. Do you need any materials that we can get for you? Like plastic or even glass for windows? Just tell us, and we'll make them for you."

They were shy about asking for things at first. Then, after a couple of them came forward to ask for cotton and string, others joined them. It wasn't long before the two of them had enough materials to help the little people do whatever they needed. And it was the most fun she'd had in a very long time.

~*~

Burton tried again to will himself to his hut. Every time he did it, he'd give himself such a headache that he needed to rest for a little bit. It bothered him that each time he tried to get home, his rest periods were taking longer and longer before he could try again. Damn it, this wasn't something that he knew how to fix.

"You there. What are you doing here?" Burton didn't bother speaking to the man that had spoken to him. He was a king, and Burton had never been one to want to associate with underlings like the man appeared to be. "Did you hear me? I asked you what you're doing here. I'm trying to run a business, and you standing in front of my stoop isn't helping me one bit."

"Be gone." The man seemed to have a death wish and grabbed him by his shoulder. "Now see here. You're not to touch me. Do you have no idea who I am? I'm the king of the Castle of Manerva. My wife…well, she's dead, but she'd have your head for touching me like this. Leave me to my magic. And be gone with you, and you're bothering me."

"Now see here. I don't know who this Manerva is, but you're in front of my shop, and I have a business to run. You're keeping people from entering here so that I can make a living." Burton tried to will himself home again and grabbed his head when it didn't work. The man, he was distracting him too much for him to concentrate. That was it. Turning to the man, he was surprised to see that it wasn't a man at all but a woman.

"Hello, Burton." He told the female that she had no right to speak to him, that he was a king of his land. "I don't really want to talk to you at all, but I was told that you were making trouble in the human world and came to make you stop it. Also, you're not the king of anything. You gave up your magic the day that I was born as your successor."

"I don't have…my daughter, you're that girl that I've been looking for. Handle, I demand that you return my magic to me. It was rightfully mine the day that your mother died. Why you lived is something that I've been looking into for some time now, but for now, I want you to — are you the reason that I cannot return to my home?" She said that her mate was. "I've heard that you've found your mate. Where is he? Perhaps the two of us can speak. Females are just too emotional. Let me speak to him, and we'll settle this as men. Like we should have long ago."

Handle looked at the man who was leaning against the building. He was a large man, much larger than he was by several feet. Burton had always been lacking in height, but he made up for it in girth. A fat king meant that he was a prosperous land owner.

"You there. I want you to have your mate get out of the castle and turn it over to me. It should have been mine in the first place. But I was tricked. They told me that I had to name her, a babe, my successor. That was a ploy to make it so that my magic was depleted. Then, they made it so that I could no longer enter my own home. Women are full of trickery and deceit. That's why they are useless for anything but fucking. Tell her to remove herself—you and I could be friends if you do what I want. It will be a wonderful feather in your hat for you to be able to tell people that you're my friend. You and I, we can make it so that there are no more females around anymore."

"Then there will be no more males born." He asked the man what he was talking about. "Women are needed for the world to be populated. Without them, well, I shudder to think what the world would be like. My own mother was good at keeping the house calming and—"

"What are you going on about? There is no need for women. Now, tell Handle here that you want her to give me back what was rightfully mine." The man looked at Handle then he did as well. "You've picked yourself a stupid one, haven't you? Someone that I can't hold a decent conversation with. Christ. I wish all women were just gone from the worlds."

"I think you've made that point quite clear. But it's not going to happen. Even if it was something that I could do, I wouldn't. And the stupidity of you thinking that there is no need for females to be around shouldn't, but it does astonish me." She sat down on a chair that hadn't been there before. Oh, to be able to do that again. To make things happen for himself with just a thought. "Your house has been removed from my lands. Also, the people that worked for you, were forced to work for you have been freed. Why did you think that anyone would be all right with you imprisoning people for your own personal gain?"

"You robbed me of my magic." He looked at the man again, finding him looking at Handle again. "Is that all he does all day is stare at you like you're some kind of…I don't know, object of beauty?"

"In the event that it might have missed your mind, she is beautiful. Kind and loving, too. I can't wait to have children with her." Burton rolled his eyes, telling the man that—

"What is your name anyway? Not that it matters all that much to me, but I might need you to do something else for me once you have Handle here out of my home. The castle is mine until I say differently." The man asked him how that had been working out for him so far. "Not well, I will admit that now. Not well at all. But now that she's here and you're going to make her do what I want, things are beginning to look up."

"I'm not going to help you, Burton. Not at all. Unless, of course, you consider the fact that I moved you off the castle land. Now, I did do that for you." Burton was so shocked by that news that he couldn't think of a single thing to say to the man. "Also, I've had the earth repaired. The damage that you did to it would have been eternal if not for the fact that you were moved off now. It's a real shame that people can't take care of the land that—did you know that there will be no more land than what we have now? We have to take care of it so that it will take care of us."

"What are you jabbering on about? Of course, there is more land. Just look over there. That's land that no one is using." He told him that it was land that was being turned into a garden for bees. "Those monsters that sting you every time you try and swat at them? Christ, that's another thing on my list of things that needs to be gotten rid of. Females and bees. I suppose the next thing that you're going to be telling me is that we need them, too."

"We do. But I'm not going to try and explain it to you. I believe that it would be a waste of my breath and time." Burton told him that was the smartest thing he'd said all day. "Yes, coming from you, that doesn't surprise me at all."

Burton asked him when he was going to tell Handle to hand over the castle and magic to him. Before he could tell him again that it was rightfully his, a group of men stood beside the chair that Handle was sitting in. Just what he needed. More people that he had to explain things to.

"Burton, I'd like for you to meet my new family. This is my mate's father and some of his brothers." He asked the man his name again. But all he did was laugh. "They're not going to give you any kind of information that you think to use against them. They're much smarter than that."

"How do I summon them then? I'm their king. I need to know that information in the event that I need something done." His own daughter laughed, telling him that he didn't have her name either. "Of course I do. You're Handle. A stupid name for sure, but I suppose it's all right for a female like you."

"Like me? What do you mean, like me?" He shrugged, telling her how useless she was. "Yes, because you believe all women need to be gone. You do know that it would be the ruination of the world should women be no more, don't you?"

"Because you say so? I don't think they have a

single use for them to even have been created for." Asking him about how babies were to come about, he stared at her for several moments and told her that he would just decree that there be babies, and that would be the end of it. "You have the power— or you think you have the power to just say there will be, I'm assuming, male babies to be around, and they'd just be there."

"No, I don't right now. Don't be stupid, Handle. I would need for you to give me my magic back for me to be able to make that happen." He looked at the other men before speaking again. "What do you think of my plans to rid the worlds of females? Can you imagine how much we'd be able to get finished? How nice it will be not to have to cater to their every whim? Every time I think of a world without women in it, I nearly jump for joy."

"Are you serious? A place where there aren't any women to be there for us? That will never fly. Oh, I suppose there would be a few men who would think that would be a good thing. But it'll never take hold. Not for me, at any rate." Burton asked the older man why he would think that. "Well, who would nurture us when we need it? Who will be there for us when we wish to have children. I don't think you just thinking that you can pop a baby in with just a thought will work. There needs to be a female around so a male can see that there are — I still, to this day, need the hug of a woman. It, for me, makes me feel like I can take on the world and win it just for them. A loving hand on my shoulders when I need a guiding hand. I'm not saying that a man couldn't do the same, raise a child on his own or with another man. But I'm saying that I need that special bond that I had with my mom. With my wife as well. And the women in my family now, including your daughter, there is something that makes me feel good about future generations coming around. You? You think you'd be better off without your momma?"

"I didn't know her, so yes, I don't think that I'd want to have her around even now." He asked him about babies. "What about them? I know how sex works and how babies are made. Yes, yes, I understand that. But I believe with all my heart that a world without women around would be a much better place."

"Would you like to see what that would mean? What your idea would mean for this world and our own?" He didn't get the chance to tell Handle that he knew what would transpire without women. It would be paradise. The place would be without strife and anger. As soon as she touched her fingers to his forehead, Burton saw what she wanted him to see.

There were women there. Not many, but there were a few. But they, too, seemed to fade out, and he had a look around at the world as he thought it would be. However, things began to change when the days turned into nights quickly. It was as if the sun and the darkness were pitted against him in his need for a world without women.

He watched as women began to fade from existence. Men were still around, he was happy to see. They were prosperous and happy. There was no anger in their voices when they spoke to one another. As the days sped by, he could see other things that changed with the fading of the female.

Men were getting older. There were no young ones around that he could see to take over jobs that were just for men. No babies for them to teach how to be someone to care for the things that were important to him. There was color still in the world, but it, too, seemed to be fading. No more bright greens of the grass. It was as if men had decided that it was beneath them to keep the cycle of life going. The few men that he saw planting trees and other vegetation soon disappeared, their gardens breaking down when there was no one there to take care of them. Burton decided that it would be something that he changed. To have men that would be the planters of the earth. Young, strong men who would care for the elderly that seemed to be in abundance.

Days passed by. Light to darkness the only marker of time. The men were now older, sickly and too frail to work the land. He also noticed that the men that had planted the earth were gone as well. Their bodies lying among the ruins of homes.

The land was barren. Not only was the earth dark and dry, but there was no color to the world at all. The few men who had been around when his vision began were now sickly, old and manic looking. Nothing, it seemed, was what he had decreed for himself when he wanted no women around.

"Where are the babes in your opinion of the world at large? There are none because you think to exclude them from ever being born. They would be there for us. The children without mothers would be just what we want, need to keep us around." Handle told him that there were no babies because the magic wasn't there to make them. There was no way for them to produce a child, carry it to term, then deliver it. "No. Not the regular way. No man will give birth—you're messing things all up with your logic. Stop it right now and show me what I want to see."

Three of the men that he'd been told were Handle's family burst out laughing. Burton asked the three of them what they'd found so funny. It took them a good ten minutes of laughter before they were able to give him an answer. It was more of the same stuff. Logical things that had no business in his new world. Things that he didn't want to think about.

After stomping off to find himself a place to think, Burton remembered that no one had given him his magic back. That his daughter hadn't turned it over like he demanded. Pissed off now, well beyond any time in his life, he used what was left of his magic to try and build him a safe haven. All he did was give himself a nosebleed and nothing else to show for his dreams.

"I'll show them. I'll figure this out and show them that there really is no need for women around when there are men that will do just as good a job—a better job than women would ever hope to achieve." It was coming on dark again when he realized that he was just too exhausted to will himself home. "I'll be going there too, by god, or I'll know the answer why."

It had made a good deal more sense in his head, but since there was no one around to correct him, Burton made himself a pillow and laid down on the ground. Damn it all to hell and back, nothing was going his way right now, and he was pissed off about it.

Chapter 2

Loren didn't move from the place he'd been sitting for the last hour or so. He wasn't sure why he was seeing what he did, but he also wasn't sure who he could tell about it either. There wasn't any way that he was going to be looking stupid in front of his family. Again. Not to mention Hanna. When a soft purr startled him away from the things in front of him, he turned to look. The large panther stretched out, showing off her claws while she was at it.

"I hope that you're Hanna." She purred and then told him that it was her. "Good. Good. That's good. I'm sort of freaking out right now. I don't know what…I was just sitting here, minding my own business, when I thought about what you said about the number seven. To be honest with you, I knew there was magic in numbers, but I only ever thought about it in terms of it being the number nine. But I'm seeing it right now that it's seven. Like it's all floating in front of me, and I have no choice but to see it. Am I making sense?"

"No. You're babbling." He glared at her and then smiled. Loren knew better than to piss off his mate. "What are you seeing that has you freaking out like a five-year-old walking through a haunted house? Which I love, by the way. Not five-year-olds. I don't hate them, but I don't know them. But I love haunted houses. Do you feel like you can explain now?"

"There are seven days to the week." She told him, kind of snarky, that she was aware of that. "Well, smart ass, did you know that there are also seven deadly sins? That there are also seven churches in the book of Revelation. Seven seals, seven trumpets and seven bowls. That the number seven is powerful in numerology as well. Not to mention—"

"Don't. Don't mention anything else. You're sounding a bit like my father right now. A little off the deep end. Calm down." Loren closed his mouth tightly and bit into his lip to keep himself from spouting off more information. "If you can tell me, how is all this information coming to you?"

He laughed and had to get a better grip on his mind. "It's in front of me. Seven-seven-seven. It's swirling around in front of me so that I can read it or understand it better." He looked at Hanna. "I'm going quite mad right now, I think. Things are not calm in my head."

"Take a deep breath." Loren thought about telling her that he'd tried that and nearly passed out when he hyperventilated. "Let it in through your nose and out your mouth, Loren. You've got this."

"No. No, I've got nothing." She turned herself into a large snake and slithered up on his lap. "You're not helping me right now. How did you think that seeing a large snake in my lap was going to make me any calmer? It's not in the event that you didn't get that."

She was suddenly on his lap, not as a snake but as a beautiful naked woman. It took him several tries to unclench his hands from the arms of the chair. Then, another five minutes of just staring at her lovely full breasts before he thought that he could speak a word without falling apart. She spoke to him then, calmly and softly.

"It's the earth telling you that the connection you have with it is there and real." Loren nodded.

"Listen to me, Loren. The earth and all the world are trying to make you understand that you're the seventh king of all the other kings that had ever been king of the shifters. Not only are you the seventh in a long line of kings, but you're also the seventh Earl of Amsterdam Castle. That's the true name of the castle where we are."

"And that's important." She told him why it was. "So I will have powerful magic that comes with being the seventh of a lot of things."

"Yes. In addition to the castle and being the earl of the lands, you're also the seventh in line for the kingdom that Aurora rules. It will never come to us just so you're aware of it, but you could be if the six people that are in line after the queen were to be killed." He nodded, his body and mind calming a bit. "You will get the magic of those six kings before you. It won't come to you with pain. I know that sometimes, when someone receives magic, it hurts. It won't from them. They understand that more than anyone else. Also, the magic that comes from defending the Castle of Amsterdam by removing my father's home from the lands here. Also, for not allowing him to enter the land. Those you did on your own, and the land knows that. How are you feeling now?"

"Better. But I did that for you, Hanna. Not for some reward." She said that the earth knew why he'd done it as well, but it made it no less important to the land. He lifted his hands up, finally relaxed enough to touch Hanna's breasts. "I'm guessing that there is a reason for you being naked and talking to me this way."

"Were you distracted enough to listen to me?" He nodded, and he leaned in and suckled at one of her nipples. "Oh yes, that's what I've got a need for. But I needed to make sure that you were going to be all right when the magic came to us."

"Later." He lifted both her breasts up and held them in front of his mouth. Suckling at them, nibbling at the tips for several minutes, he asked her what kind of magic. "I mean, is it something that can be put off for a little while?"

"Yes, I think so—oh Loren, you need to be naked." He was. Just willing his clothing away so that he could fulfill her wish. "I need you to be inside of me. Now, if you would."

Loren nearly came when she adjusted herself around until she was seated over him. Christ, it was like sticking his dick in a furnace, it felt that hot. But wonderful at the same time. Each time Hanna rocked toward him, he would bite again on her nipple and suckle at one of them hard. Watching as they bounced and jiggled was fascinating to him. As her riding became more frantic, more out of sync with his own movements, she held onto his hair and pulled him to her breasts.

Pulling her toward him again, cupping her warm, firm orbs that were her ass to him, he felt the moment that she came. Her sheath tightened around his cock, her body stiffened, and when she screamed, holding onto him in a tight, painful grip, it was all he could do not to come with her.

Taking them to the master bedroom, he was thrilled to see that the bed was large. Big enough for her body and his, too. Laying her down over the mattress, he continued to fuck her as he did her mouth with his tongue. Christ, he thought, he was never going to be the same after this and found that he really didn't care.

Hanna came several more times. Hard, like punches to his system, reminded him that he'd not come yet. His body needed to please her more before he could release. When she bit down on his shoulder, not just breaking skin but bones as well, Loren threw back his head and howled out his release as his wolf, ever-present nowadays, seemed to come at the same time with their mate.

Waking alone in the bed, he reached out for Hanna. She was just in the bathroom, and when she came to him, like a specter in the darkness, he wasn't the least bit surprised when she saddled him again, his cock finding a home inside of her that he wanted to remain forever. As she fucked him with her body, he explored her with his own.

Loren found scars along her ribs that he was going to ask her about later. Small indentations that made her sigh when he touched them. Using his tongue at her throat, he nibbled on her ear lobes, then her throat and neck, as he found more places that he'd not touched earlier. Rolling her to her back, still deep inside of her, Loren put her hands above her head and held them there.

He took her as he watched her face. Loren could tell when she was close to coming again, and he'd slow himself down. When she was needing more, he would give it to her, but only to a point. Then he'd take it away. As soon as he felt her climax taking her, he pulled back, trying his best to make it last for them both.

Her body moved. Adjusted to his in a way that had him seeing stars. Even as he slowed his pace, something moved over him. Time seemed to have no meaning for him as he stood on the ledge of limbo, his own body pausing for what he knew was going to be an epic release, one for all time.

He never expected to come when he did. As his body was filling hers, over and over, releasing into her heat, he held onto her tightly, knowing that on some level that, if he didn't, he was going to shatter into a million and one pieces. As it was, hanging on to her was all that he had left in his mind.

Waking in the large bed, he knew that all he had to do was put out his hand to touch Hanna. But his body, spent like he'd never had before, couldn't move. Not even the few inches that were between the two of them. Hearing her giggle didn't help either. He was that wasted. Knowing that he was completely drained of even one ounce of energy. Closing his eyes, he let his exhaustion take him.

Rolling over, he knew that it was late enough in the day that he should have been up hours ago. Not that he cared right now. When he sat up in the bed, he looked around the room he was in. As far as he was concerned, it was perfect. Just what he'd pick out for a master bedroom in a castle.

Standing up, holding onto the bed posts for support, he gingerly made his way to the bathroom and looked at himself in the mirror. Just as he was turning to turn on the shower, he noticed something about his arm. About his whole body, really. He was much larger than when he'd awakened yesterday.

His muscles were well-defined. Loren knew that he was in good shape, but now he looked like he could lift a car and not break a sweat. His neck was thicker as well. Standing back, he tried to get a sense of his entire body when Hanna came into the room. She, too, looked more fit than she had before.

"What's going on?" After explaining to her what he was seeing. She turned the small mirror over the sink into one that they could both see their bodies in front of. "I am larger. Like I've been hit up with some muscle juice."

"They call that milk, moron. But I think you're right. Both of us have been beefed up a bit." When she was suddenly as naked as he was, his cock stretched, but he ached too. Laughing when she told him she too was sore, they got into the shower together without any hanky panky, Hanna called it.

They were making the bed haphazardly

when Hanna told him of the things that they had to do today. It was a running list, she told him, in no certain order. When he was dressed and ready to face whatever the day brought, he sat down on the chest at the end of the bed and watched as Hanna stared out the window near their bed.

"What is it?" Hanna told him that she wasn't sure. "Is it your father? I know that I have to deal with him today. For some reason, it came to me just now that he's going to be my responsibility from now on. I don't mind at all just so you know. Anything to keep you from being hurt by him."

"Thank you for that." Hanna turned and looked at him. "The meetings that we have with Aurora aren't going to be quick. She's going to reward Andy, the man that I worked with at the restaurant. I've talked to her about it. I believe that he would be too overwhelmed if she were to give him a great deal of money. And she was. He'll feel as if what he did was in the name of friendship, and that is what she's going to be telling him. That saving her friend was important to her."

"That might make it easier on him, but I think he'll be no less overwhelmed." Hanna told him she didn't think that he would be either. "What else will this meeting take care of with her? I have a feeling that she's going to give something to my dad and brothers. Is that it?"

"Aurora told me that she's been trying to reward your family for decades, and you won't have it. She said that she's going to lump all the thank yous into one gift, and they'll have to take it. For helping to save me." Hanna rolled her eyes, and he had to laugh. "Now that I've met your family, I can tell that they'd put up a fuss if she only rewarded them a nickel. But this will be so much more."

"My dad has always said that what we do for her is in the name of the earth itself. I'm sure that it's not going to be a minor fuss either." She laughed as he had hoped that she would. "What is it that you're not telling me? Is it something to do with us being mates?"

"A great deal." She came and sat on his lap, facing him. It was his favorite new position of holding his lovely mate. "As the queen and now you as the king of shifters, I've never been paid. I should have been. Annually, money comes to the people in charge of an area that we watch over for her, like us and the shifters. We are rules, and she compensates us. Well, she's not me yet. I think that now that she has me cornered, and she does, I'm going to receive what I should have been getting for years and years."

"I'm assuming that it's more than we can carry out in our pockets." She nodded. "Like a lot more than a pocket full?"

"More like this castle full." He was still sitting there when she came and smacked him in the face. Looking at her, at her beauty, all he could think about was how fucking huge this castle was. Getting up when she pulled him along behind her, Loren was afraid that he was going to be crushed by what her payment was going to be.

~*~

Burton didn't think that it was fair that he'd been summoned to the castle of Aurora like he was nothing more than some minion that was going to be punished. There were rules, and Aurora wasn't following protocol like she should have done with him. An invitation should have been sent out. He would have to reply if he was coming or not and how many would be in his party. Then, it would be sent directly back.

Rarely did he do things *directly* or in any kind of quick way. He preferred to make the person that had sent out the invite to stew about their inviting him to their home. Also, he would send out spies to figure out who else had been invited to whatever was going on. This telling invite to him to get his ass there — exactly what the invite had said and not to be late pissed him off.

There was no mention of a car coming to get him. Nothing was said about food or drink. He was near starving to death as it was. And had no clean clothing. Burton liked to attend these things dressed to the hilt. In a way that had others, all of the others at the palace, talking about what he was wearing and who he came with. Not this time, however.

It took him nearly two hours to figure out how he was supposed to arrive. It was the man, supposed to be mated to his daughter, Handle. He'd just shown up where he was standing and told him to shut up and get into the car. It wasn't even a limo but a pickup truck that looked dusty and dirty. No one respected their elders like they should anymore.

"What is this all about?" He didn't answer him. "Do you hear me? I've asked you a question, and as your supposed father-in-law, you are required to answer me. Why have I been summoned here today? Doesn't she know that I have more important things to do than—"

"You mean stealing food from the grocery store? Or do you think that trying to sleep in the library is a good thing to be known for?" Burton told the man he hadn't any idea what his name was, nor did he care, that his daughter had made it so that he couldn't live in his home that belonged to him. "I sent you away from our lands, not your daughter. Also, I made it so that you couldn't enter the lands again as well. It's amazing the kind of things you can do when you have a lot of magic, isn't it? Oh, I forgot, you have very little. Certainly enough, I would imagine that you could bathe once in a while. You stink."

"I do not stink, young man. I don't like taking baths, and — why is it that someone yammers on and on about bathing? It's not healthy, you know. To sit in the water while it clouds up." The man told him that a person was to wash their body, not soak in a tub to be clean. "Whatever. I do what I want because I am king. And you'd best be learning that, too. I would hate to have my daughter a widow before a child comes along. Not that I want anything calling me grandda." He shivered at the thought. "Christ. Do not make me a grandfather. I will not allow it."

"Since it would be none of your business if we were to have fifty children, you won't be consulted about it. Now. We're going to have this meeting with the queen. You're to listen to what she has to say to you, and then you will do what she wants of you." Burton tsked. "I'm serious here, Burton. I will harm you if you put up any kind of argument. You've been told enough times that this day was coming. You will do as you're told, or I will take you to task."

"You? You think that you're going to take me to anything?" He pointed out that he was taking him to the meeting. "Don't be a smart ass. I know that. It's as it should be. That you're the one picking me up. I would have preferred a nice limo. But I'm sure that it's out of your price range to have one just sitting around waiting for you to have me picked up."

"My family has three limos, as a matter of fact." Again, Burton rolled his eyes. "Believe me or not, Burton, I could care less. However, you cause shit today, and I'll take care that you never see the light of day again. I will put you in a prison so deep and dark, you'll never know the passing of years, much less days."

"Like you have any say in things like this." Burton decided that he wasn't going to allow his daughter any time with this man. He was a tyrant, and he didn't like him. "I have the ear of my daughter.

When I see her today, she will be there, I'm told. I'll tell her how you treated me, and we'll see how things go with that. You're not fit to be her servant, much less her mate."

"Tell me, Burton. What is her name? Or mine, for that matter. Not that you have to know my name, but you should know your daughters. I know the circumstances of their birth, too. The way that you killed her sisters. Two little girls that could have been a comfort in your olden age. How even though the wind knocked your wife off her feet, you could have saved her but simply offering your hand to her." He didn't speak to the man. Not that he really wanted to, but Burton thought that he knew entirely too much information. "You didn't even know that your oldest lived either. Because once she was taken away from the birthing room, you never saw her again until she was ready to rule her kingdom. What is her name, Burton? Do you even remember your wife's name? I do. Queen Shannon. Retired Queen of all Shifters, Dame of Castle Manerva, mother to Hanna, current Queen of all Shifters. My mate."

"For now." Burton laughed. "You don't even know the name of your own mate, you idiot. Her name…I've forgotten what you called her, but she is

Handle, my daughter."

"Her name is Hanna, you fucking bastard." The man stopped the car so suddenly that Burton hit his head on the dash. Once they were going again, he felt blood seeping down over his eyes. "You need to get your shit together, you mother fucker, so that you can face the consequences of your actions."

He opened the door and got out. Looking around, seeing if the little prick had left him in the middle of nowhere, he was surprised to see that they were in front of a lovely home. One that he thought he could make his own. Getting out, dusting the imaginary dust off his sleeves, Burton set his mind to working on how he was going to have someone turn this house over to him. It would make the perfect set up for him until he was back in the castle. Yes, sir, he thought, Handle or whatever she told the young man her name was when he knew better, was going to pay the piper, as it were.

Burton entered the house like he owned it already. There were others around the massive rooms. Smelling something that made his belly rumble a bit, he followed the scents to a layout of food that made him have to pause and take a deep breath; it looked so good. Picking up one of the many golden plates, he was surprised to find that they were made of something other than gold, he began piling it high with foods that he found.

There were vegetables there as well as fruits, but he bypassed those for the meaty portions that were on the platters. He'd never liked when hosts would lay out a large dining experience only to have things like that on it. Who in their right mind would eat fruits and vegetables when there were so many other delights to have? No one, that was who. Burton would chastise his wife for doing something like this. But she would do it every time. He would never understand the workings of a woman's mind.

"Is that you, Burton?" He didn't bother looking at the person who had spoken to him but said that he was. "I thought as much. My goodness, if you don't mind me saying so, you've lost a bit of weight, haven't you? Must be because you're no longer king. Gorging yourself on other people's dinners has made you almost fit." He turned to look at the woman. Burton didn't have any idea who she was and didn't bother speaking to her. He did, however, push her out of his way of the sweets.

Burton was on his way to get a second plate to fill up when he saw Handle. It was hard for him to decide if he wanted to talk to her or not. But he did in the end, thinking that it would be nice of him to go and tell her that her mate or whatever he was calling himself had her name wrong. Idiot. Also, he decided to let her have the opportunity to hand over his magic without having to start any inquiries about her actions in taking it from him.

"Hello, daughter." She just stared at him without saying a word. "Don't be like that. I just came here to tell you that the idiot that you're supposed to be mated to is calling you by the wrong—"

"My name is Hanna Tate. Not Handle. Why on earth would you think that someone would be calling their child a part of a pan? Hanna. Say it with me. Hanna Tate. And don't get too comfortable, either. I'm here to have you put away." He didn't bother with telling her that she in no way was going to do anything to him when he asked her for his magic back. "I know that I have to hand it over to you willingly. However, I'm not going to. I have no desire to give you anything. Once today is over with, you'll be out of my life for good."

"You're being highly disrespectful. I won't stand for it, Handle." Burton decided that he was going to call her that regardless of what she said. "I was tricked into handing it over to you, and I will not speak to you again until you see reason. I liked being king. I was good at it. I never bothered anyone, and no one bothered me. I had all the magic that I wished for, plus food and lovely clothing. You'll do as you're told."

"Then it wouldn't be willingly now, would it? Making me hand my magic over to you wouldn't be—oh, never mind. You're not going to be king again. Loren is." He asked who that was. "My mate. The man who brought you here. Do you ever pay attention to what people say to you?"

"I do not. Not unless it's something that I wish to hear. Now, I want you to do right by me and hand the magic back to me. It's the least you can do for all the trouble that you've caused me. Why would you think that it was right of you to lock me out of my own home? Not to mention, leave me with nothing more than pickings of things when I'm a man used to luxury and the finer things in life." She asked him what she was supposed to do if she were to hand over the magic. "What do I care what you do with your life after I am king again? You'll be lucky if I don't turn you into the queen for what all you have done to me."

"We'll see." Then she had the nerve to walk away from him. As if he were nothing at all to her. Had it not been for his grumbling belly, he would have gone after her. But he decided to find himself a nice corner and eat until he was stuffed.

Just as he was sitting down, the meeting was called to order. Not only did his plates of food disappear, but the large table of food disappeared as well. Damn it all to hell and back. No one was treating him the way that he deserved today. Standing up, he went to find out who was in charge of this catastrophe. Surely, someone would figure out that he should have been treated better than they were.

By the time he was able to figure out where all the things had gone, the staff had put it all away. He tried to tell them that he was an important person and would need to be treated differently, but all they kept telling him was that they had a job to do. Burton wished that his own staff was set on doing what they'd been told to do all the time. There was a good chance he'd not be in the predicament that he was in now, that was for sure.

"Burton, what are you doing?" He asked Aurora what she was about. "I'm starting the meeting, and you're disrupting the staff. Come sit down with everyone else, and we'll begin."

"Why is it that I must sit with—don't you have a special place for people like me to sit? I think that me sitting with the commoners is not right." Aurora told him to sit down and shut up. "I don't like this. Not one bit."

"I don't care." She took in several deep breaths before speaking again. "All right. Today, I have several things on my list to take care of. But first of all, I wish to thank Loren and Hanna for agreeing to host this thing—"

"Her name is Handle." Everyone turned to look at him. "You would think that for as old as you were that you'd get her name correct. It's Handle."

"It's Hanna, you fool. Now shut up and listen." Aurora did threaten him again with putting tape over his mouth if he didn't shut up. Waving her off, knowing that she'd not embarrass herself like that, he stood along the wall with the guards rather than sit with the commoners. "I've several things that I wish to address today. I'm going to start with the good things and make my way to the things that are a nuisance."

Some of the people seated turned and looked at him, but he ignored them as best he could. Usually,

Burton didn't mind being singled out on things, but today was different. He wasn't at his best and didn't get to dress up. He put another thing on his list in his head that he was going to make sure never happened again.

While Aurora went on about some man named Andy and his help in saving Hanna, he thought about the first things that he was going to do when he was reinstated as king. First and foremost, he was going to make sure that no one, not even by blood, could enter the castle or anywhere else he was without his written permission. That was right below making sure that he had a clean and tailored suit for every day. He did want to look his best at all times. Even if he had to simply go out and inspect something. But surely he'd be able to find someone to do that for him, too. The applauding brought him from his thoughts, and he wasn't happy about it.

"Now for the other items on my list." He wasn't thrilled about being here when it seemed that nothing was about him. Then Aurora turned to him. "Burton, former king of the shifters, would you please come stand before me?"

"Why?" She just glared at him. "Look. I've things to say myself. My daughter isn't treating me well. I'd like for you to do something about it."

"I am. That's why I want you to come stand before me." Smiling, he was happy that things were finally getting on the right path. Why, to his way of thinking, he'd be back in his castle before nightfall. Almost giddy, he made his way to stand before Aurora. "Loren and Hanna? If you would be so kind as to come up here too."

"Thank you for this, Aurora. It's taken you long enough to get your head out of your ass to make this happen, but I guess I can't be too picky. You are just a woman, after all." He looked at his daughter and her so-called mate. "You're going to have to listen to me from now on, daughter. And don't think I've forgotten what you've done to me either. You're going to pay for your treatment of me. See that I'm right."

"You really think so?" Nodding, he looked at Aurora when she said his name again. "You'd better be paying attention, father. I don't think that anything is going to go your way anytime too soon."

Smiling at Aurora, he hoped she'd get the hint that she was to get this over with. It had been long in coming to him, his way of life returned to him. When Aurora asked him if he had anything to say about what she'd just said to him, he looked around the room and then back at her.

"Damn it, woman. Why do you keep talking to me when I'm not paying attention? Just repeat what you said and I'll give you my answer. And I'm telling you right now, I'm not going to budge one bit on you making sure that I have everything that I deserve." She told him that he'd get that and more. "Now. Right there. That's the way to make people happy. You don't even have to repeat yourself. I'm agreeing to the terms you set up. Oh, doggy. I'm going to be as happy as a bed bug. You just wait and see."

"So you don't need me to tell you what I said about you?" He said that he was ready to move on. "You're sure? I don't want to have you coming back on me and saying that you didn't understand. You're only going to get one shot at this."

"I'm as sure as I am happy." He looked at Handle. "You hear that? This will be the last time I have to put up with your ever taking shit from me again."

Chapter 3

Loren laughed every time he thought of Burton's face when he was sentenced for the murders of his family. Not that he was going to serve any time in a jail or prison. But he'd been stripped of his immortality. Not to kill him right away but so that he would age like any other human—as he was now—and die of old age. Well, in his case, older age.

"Are you still getting a good laugh out of Burton?" He nodded at Hanna and smiled at her when she admitted that she was as well. "He seriously thought that I was going to be the one that would be in trouble. Not to mention how he'd put out his hand when Aurora had talked about the castle property like I was going to have to turn it over to him right then. What a dumb ass."

"I forgot to ask, but other than me telling her what I'd seen in Burton's mind about how Shannon and your sisters had been killed, how did she figure out the evidence? I mean, so far as I know, the only way to have had any was to have gone back in time and recorded it. Right?" Hanna sat down in his office chair while he continued to put files into the newly arrived cabinet. "Can Aurora do that?"

"Not that I know of. However, she can use that as evidence since it was so long ago, and there wouldn't be any recordings of anything like that. It frustrated her too that when my mother fell to her death from the castle turret, she landed on stones rather than the soft grass. I don't know that it would have kept her from dying. But it would have given her a fighting chance. Aurora also thinks that even though Burton didn't push her, his intentions were the same as he'd lured her to the top of the castle, knowing full well that she was going to be having trouble with it. She was at the end of her pregnancy. That was more than likely his plan all along. To murder her before the children were born." Loren asked if there was a reason for him doing that. Before she'd been born. "Yes. Without a spouse or children to take over for him after we died, then he would be ruler for life. That would have been a major disaster. The kingdom would have surely fallen into ruin if that would have happened, and I think that everyone knew it. The few years that he was in charge until I was old enough to take over the position was certainly cause for concern. It's why he was made to resign when he did. If the shifters were in trouble for any reason, even if they weren't able to find food — which likely would have been the case — the entire species of shifters would have been lost to the world."

"Christ, I never thought of that. Even now, there are more shifters than there are wholly wolves, I believe. To not have them around would have been, just as you said, a disaster." He smiled then, thinking of some of the things that Burton had said to them. "He honestly thought that with you in charge that there would be no more males born. The man is an idiot thinking that one sex or the other could have survived without the opposite sex."

"Yes, well, I heard that every day I was around him. How there was no need for women to be around. I haven't any idea how he thought that was going to work out for the world. But that's my father for you." She leaned back in the chair. "I wonder how he's fairing today. It would have been a strange night for him. Without magic, he wouldn't have had the comforts of a bed or even a roof over his head.

That would have been just too terrible for him. Not that I care."

When the doorbell sounded, he waited to see who it was before going to the hall. Having staff had saved him a great deal of time in not having to deal with people coming around with their hand out. Since he was working from home today, Loren knew that most of the people he didn't want to talk to would go home after finding the office closed up. A few, very few, he hoped, knew where he lived and would come here.

"Lady Hanna. It's your father." She asked Jules what he wanted. "He says for you to come to him that, and I quote, he's 'in too much bloody pain' to come up the stairs. I do believe that he walked here from town."

Loren walked with Hanna. He wasn't going to miss anything about Burton if it would give him a good laugh. It would be a great story to tell his family later. Hanna stopped suddenly and glared at him. Asking what had happened, she crossed her hands over her breasts and glared harder at him.

"You will not be the one telling the story this time. You laugh too much, and they get bored waiting on you to get to the end." He kissed her on the nose and told her that it was just too funny. "Yes. But I'm going to tell them about whatever he wants. He is my sire, after all."

"All right. But next time, it will be me. We have to share in his woes so that we can both get to tell them. You have to admit, honey, that it usually turns out to be the best stories that are told." She turned on her heel, and he followed her. "I'm going to take notes. So that we—you don't forget something funny."

They were at the door together when he spotted Burton. The man did look as if he was in a good deal of pain. Standing on the walkway, he was leaning heavily on a large stick that looked to be too weak to hold him. His hair, usually so neatly combed and styled do to magic, had a messiness about it that didn't look good on the old man. He sat down on the stairs to watch the exchange between Burton and his daughter. Remembering what he said to Hanna, he did pull out a note pad and pen to take notes.

"What do you want now? I thought that it had been made perfectly clear to you that you weren't to bother me again about me giving you magic. You were told that you had to live out your days on your own." Burton nodded at Hanna, Loren just realizing that Burton didn't have on any shoes and his feet were muddy. "If you know that, then why the hell are you here? I have better things to do than to—"

"Daughter, I'm in pain." Loren got up to investigate. He didn't like the man, but there was no reason for him to suffer if he'd hurt himself. "I had to walk to the empty building there that I was staying. My feet were hurting so bad. No one is meant to walk like this. Why, I never in all my days had my feet feel like they've been put on a bed of nails. I've always been hungry for my next meal almost as soon as I get up from the table. However, it seems now that my belly is making up for lost time and making such a noise that I can't sleep at night. Then there's that. Sleeping. Good Christ. I need my magic back. I won't bother you, but I need to have—I couldn't make me a nice fluffy mattress. I had stones as my pillows. It's not right for a man to have to suffer as I have been. Oh! And don't get me started on the noises that come from my bottom. It's absolutely revolting the sounds and smells that come—someone told me it was gas. It's more like the noxious smells that come from a dead body. You have to help me, Hanna. I can't do this. You shouldn't want me to do this."

"You made your bed, yes, pun intended. Now,

you must lie in it. I've no doubt that you're suffering. I want you to think of the suffering that you caused me when you killed my mother and sisters. It's far worse than—" Burton stiffened up.

Both he and Hanna took a few steps back when Burton's *bottom*, as he called it, let go of the loudest and most horrific noise and smell he'd ever smelled. Hanna was gagging, and he had to pull his shirt up and over his nose so none of the gas accidentally got into his mouth. It was putrid.

"Now, do you see what I mean? Christ, it's like my bottom is rotted from the inside out. I can't stand this anymore." He wasn't going to open his mouth to tell him to leave the area before he killed their poor trees. Loren thought that since Hanna wanted this story, he was going to let her have it. Walking back to the porch, he sat down, still covering his mouth. "What do you mean, I have to deal with this on my own. I won't have it."

Loren wondered for a moment if Burton had let go of another gaseous emission, but Hanna seemed to be all right. At least she was still upright for now. When she told her father that he was going to have to watch what he ate from now on or he'd be like this forever, Burton looked as if he was going to sob.

"I don't want to watch what I eat. I want my magic so that I don't have—people are running from me, Handle. When I have this noise problem, they run away. Screaming. One little girl told me that I was vile. I most certainly wasn't vile before you and that damned queen took my magic from me." He looked down at himself, and Loren did the same. He really was a mess. "Just look at me. I'm wearing the same clothing that I had on two days ago. And it's taken on the odor of the noise. What is that called anyway." Loren laughed when she told her father. He refused to believe her.

"Well, that's what it's called. Fart. Haven't you ever heard the saying, like a fart in the wind? Well, that's what you're doing. Farting in the wind. However, if I were you, I'd do it when the wind is blowing away from people. You might just kill someone by getting too close to them when you let that crap go." Her father wasn't amused, but he was. Christ, Loren thought he'd be laughing for the rest of his life thinking about his mate teaching her father about farts. "Another thing that you'll have to do— though I know you're not going to like it—you're going to need to take a bath more often. If you think that your farts are bad, wait until you mix a little body odor with it. You'll never be able to enter any establishment again. They'll toss you—no. No one would touch you. That's about how bad it is now. You stink."

"Stop saying that. I do not stink." Hanna nodded, and Loren had to stifle a laugh when Burton stomped his foot. "Well, I don't. And if you would just hand over my magic again, I'll not have to put up with the stares I'm getting. It's not fair that I have to be seen like this."

"You love it when people stare at you." Burton shouted that he didn't when he wasn't dressed properly. "I don't know what to tell you. Other than the fact that you do indeed stink. That you're only going to get smellier as time goes on, and you're not getting any magic. You did this to yourself, and I'm—"

"There is no way that you will believe that I did this to myself." This time, when he let gas go, he actually lifted his leg up and moaned when he was finished. "I'll only admit this to you now, but my belly gets very full feeling, then when I let some of this smell go, I do feel a bit better. But I don't like it. Nor you. I cannot for the life of me figure out why you won't help me. I'm your father."

"Yes, you are. But I don't like you. Nor do I respect you. You not only killed my mother but my sisters as well. What sort of excuse do you have for that." Burton stomped his foot again before telling Hanna why he'd killed them. "Just as I thought. You killed them for their birthright. Well, how does it feel knowing that it was all for nothing? That you're no more king than the rocks beneath your feet are."

"It's not fair." Hanna looked back at him and then back at her father. She said the words that she told him that she would say to her father, given the chance. "What are you talking about? You know as well as I do that I can't bring your mother and sisters back. They're nothing but dust now. That isn't even a good trade. Tell me something else that you'll take from me for magic. Something easy, if you please. I don't want to have to walk or do much for you to trade me, even for magic. Come on. Why don't you tell me that I'm to give you…I don't know. My shirt. I'll be cold, but only for a bit. Once you give me my magic back, then I can just make me another one."

When he started to unbutton his shirt, Hanna turned and walked toward him. Burton kept telling her to wait on him; he was nearly finished, but she sat down beside him and buried her face in his shoulder.

Loren looked at Burton when he was still a few feet away.

"That's close enough." Burton said they were trading. "No. She never said that. You did. And we were told by Aurora not to give you magic. That you have to live out your days as a human. And that is less than I think you deserve for killing three people. You're lucky that she didn't charge you with all the other deaths that we know about. It's my understanding that they've found a great many faeries buried on the land that you were on. I would have charged you for each of their deaths, too, and sentenced you to death by them. I have heard that they have the most fun when told to kill someone that has taken the life of their own."

"They're not nice. Never once did they help me out when I ordered them to." Loren told the man that he didn't have the right to order anyone around. "So you say. But I was a king, and while I wasn't all that good at it, I enjoyed myself. What king wouldn't?"

"I won't take advantage of any creature that is in my care." Burton said he was a sap then. "Yet there you stand with blistered feet, dirty clothing and no food, telling me how much you want magic to benefit yourself. I will not do that. And I made a promise to Aurora and myself that I wouldn't either. Together, Hanna and I are going to be good to the people that we were meant to help. We'll work hard in keeping them safe, too."

"So? You don't think that I didn't do that?" Loren said that he'd not. "Okay, so maybe I didn't. But as I said, I did have a good time. And I'm betting that you will as well. In a few days, you're going to realize how much fun you can have with magic. Not to mention how much it will benefit you to have it. I wouldn't have ever left the castle hadn't it been for your mate, HANDLE, making me do that."

"Hanna. Her name is Hanna." Burton just shook his head, saying that he knew better. "Whatever you say. But I want you gone from here. And you're never return. You've pissed me off enough for one afternoon, and I don't want to have to deal with your shit or smell any longer. Be gone, Burton."

He didn't even care enough to wonder where the man had disappeared to. Lifting Hanna's chin up, he looked into her tear-filled eyes. If he didn't know better, he'd swear —

"You're laughing." She nodded and rolled away from him to the ground, her body tight with her humor. "I thought all this time he'd upset you, and you were crying. Damn it, woman. You scared me."

"Christ, he actually was going to give me that stupid smelly shirt. Oh, Loren, I don't know how you were able to stand there. Even with my nose covered, it was more than I could handle." He rolled to the ground, too, and started tickling her. "Don't. Please don't. I'll pee myself."

The two of them were still on the ground, laughing, when his dad showed up. It took them both twenty minutes to make him understand why they were there and laughing so hard. Even handing him his notes that he'd taken with a shaky hand from laughing didn't help him understand. There were days, like today, that he thought life was the best. Then, with his new mate and his family so close, it was better than his life could have ever been arranged for him. Loren was in love. With life, his family and his wonderfully humorous wife, too.

~*~

Hanna had to keep herself in check. Even the slightest thought of her father had her giggle. It wasn't appropriate today. She was having court for some of the shifter issues that had been going on. Even though it did help to know that she could still laugh after all the crap — again, she was in peals of laughter before catching herself.

"Madam Tate?" Waving the man off who was standing in front of her table asked her again if she was all right. "You seem to be a little confused about what the man next to me has been doing."

"No. No, you're right. I do understand, but I'm having an off day. Nothing that will, I promise you, interfere with my verdict of what I'm seeing here. Go on. Tell me what else Mr. Levi has been doing to your farm."

"He's been teaching his children how to chase after my chickens as their little beasts. I know I said this before to you, but they are little beasts. They run through my wife's flowers, throwing them around like heathens. Then, if that wasn't bad enough, they scared my poor goats to badly that they won't milk anymore. I can't have that, my lady. I feed my family with my animals. They can't survive, and neither can we if he keeps at this." Mr. Levi said they were having just a bit of fun. "It's not fun to my animals. They're destroying my livelihood." She asked Levi if he had anything to say.

"I don't know why he came to you with his. It's just a bit of kids having some fun. Sure, they did tear

up the flowers, but I told them not to do it anymore."
She asked him if they had stopped. "Well, no. But
they're just kids." He looked at her hard, and she had
a feeling that he was going to tell her it was his right.
"Your daddy. He'd of not even bothered with this.
This is just like the kind of thing that he didn't want
to be bothered with. I don't know why you didn't
just let him be king. He was a good king, and I never
had nary a bit of trouble before this."

"Because there was no one around to take you
to task before." He agreed with her and told her
that she should be doing the same. "I don't think so.
You're fined three years in jail doing hard labor. Or
you can work for Mr. Brown, helping him get his
farm back to the way it was."

"I don't want to work. See, that's another thing
he wouldn't have done. Made someone work for
what they did. I don't want to go to jail, either. I have
me some daytime television that I've got to keep up
on. Not to mention, me and my misses, we have stuff
to do at home too."

Hanna asked Mrs. Levi to stand. Then asked her
if she had a job. When she got her answer that no, she
didn't. She asked her why neither of them worked.
It seemed as if no one in the area was working for a

living.

"We get those nice benefits from the humans. They give us a food card and a discount on a lot of stuff. Like me and Levi here, we don't pay anything for our electricity bill. And we pay no rent either on account of us being so broke all the time. Even taking us to the doctor don't cost us nothing. I think it was your daddy that told us to sign up for the stuff. He was a good king." Hanna asked her how they paid for their kids' clothing and food for lunches and such, ignoring the fact that she made it clear about how she thought of her ruling the lot of them. "Oh, we get all that for free, too. I still have a list of places that we hit up when they have stuff to give away. It's not as easy as it used to be to get things for free anymore. Like they limit you on the amount of stuff you can take out. But we have us a system on that, too. I go, then Levi, he goes too. We each take a couple of our kids with us to let them see that we're not mooching off them. And if you're going to suggest we get a job, well, you might want to know that it messes with our income. They don't want you to work if you're getting help from them."

"But you are mooching off of them, Dawn. You both are. It's also doubtful to me that they have suggested that you don't get a job. I'm betting that they're hoping you get one so that you don't have to have *assistance* — which is what it is, assistance — anymore." She told her that she didn't see it that way. "Yes, but I do. And I'm going to be putting a stop to it right now." Hanna looked around the room before standing up and clearing her throat. "How many of you are on welfare? Getting food and or insurance from the county?"

Nearly everyone in the room held up their hands. And she would bet that nearly every one of them were also causing trouble too. They had too much time on their hands and were getting into things just to have something to do. Hanna was going to fix that as well.

While she understood that some of the people on the program did really need it. She also knew that there were more than double that number of people that were taking advantage too. Like Dawn and Levi were. This was something that she and Loren had talked about last night.

"Starting as soon as tomorrow, if you don't have a good sound reason and an excuse from a reputable doctor as to why you are on the governmental programs, you will get a job." The grumblings were getting louder with each word she spoke. "I will be back in two weeks. When I come back, you will each and every one of you will be working or starting to work. You'll be *assisted* with housing as well as food for the first few months after having a job. Then, after a reasonable time, I expect you to be able to stand on your own two feet."

"Now that's not fair. You're not being fair to us." She asked Levi how it was fair for him not to be working. "I don't want to work. It's too stressful, and it takes up most of my day to have a job. Then there is all that trouble of trying to get there on time. Following the rules? No, I don't want to work. It's just too easy not to have to do anything than it is to work all day long. You change that rule right now."

She stood up, and when she did, all the men in the room did as well. Hanna wasn't worried about them. Not at all. What she was worried about was how badly they were going to be hurting when she called for help. Putting her fingers into her mouth, she let out a shrill whistle, and the doors behind her burst inward. Hanna didn't have to turn and look to see the large group of faeries that were behind her.

"This is my army. They do what I tell them to do." No one moved. Levi looked like he was even trying hard not to blink. "Each of you will have one of my army faeries help you in your finding time to get a job and keeping it. If I hear that any of you have harmed or refused to work with them, I will remove your head where you stand. Do I make myself clear?"

Just to show them how much she wanted this to happen, with a snap of her fingers, the building that they were in disappeared. As did the chairs, tables and anything else that was there for them to use. They huddled to the middle of the room, wide-eyed and terrified looking, when they realized that they were fucking with the wrong person. The faeries circulated around the room, then two and three of them going to each person in the room.

Hanna had already spoken to the group of faeries that were there for her and Loren to use. They knew how to help those who were needing the help to get more assistance if they needed it and to keep on top of the ones that were milking the system. Loren was doing the same thing on the other end of the state to the shifters there, taking advantage of the people of the town they were in. She thought this was a great way to make sure that they were not just working but keeping out of trouble, too. She looked at Levi and Mr. Brown.

"Levi, you will send your sons to work with Mr. Brown. If they don't do what he tells them to do, then I will rain shit down on them that they'll never recover from. Understand?" He nodded like his neck was broken. "Mr. Brown, you will be compensated for your chickens as well as your goats. Also, so long as the boys are working for you and doing a good job, the Tate foundation will pay their wages. But only if they're doing a good job. All right?"

"Yes, ma'am." Mr. Brown smiled at her. "Yes, ma'am, I understand a few things right now. You're not a pushover, not that I ever thought you'd be one, and you're a mate to one of them Tate boys. Yes. I'll make them work. You'll see that too when you come back here. I'll make them into good boys by realizing that everything in life isn't free."

She didn't even bother telling him that he'd have faeries with him to help. When he left the building, four of the ones who had farming knowledge went out the door working. Hanna turned to Levi and Dawn. They still had things that they were doing that were against the shifter laws.

"Starting tomorrow, both of you will show up at the shelter where you've been getting food from. You'll both work eight hours a day handing out food and other items that are needed by the patrons that go there." Dawn said she had things to do. "Tough shit. You'll be there or be dead. I'm done with the two of you and what you've been up to right under our noses. I've heard about the shit that the two of you have been doing, and I'm putting a stop to that as well. Your drug dealing days are finished. So is the car stealing and reselling that you've been doing for money, too. You'll no longer be welcome to put names on the Christmas trees in the fall. There will be no more freebies at restaurants when you go there. The very fact that the two of you have been hurting other businesses by your actions is enough for me to sentence you to prison, shifter prison. Also, and this one thrills me to no end. As of right now, you no longer have housing. You have been moved into a house more suited to your income."

"We don't want to move out. Damn it. You're picking on us, and I don't like it." She told Levi that she didn't care. "Well, you will when I'm finished with you."

The gun, which she'd known he had, disappeared as soon as he pulled it out of the back of his pants. In less time than it had taken him to pull the gun, he was dead. The faeries had done their job in protecting her. Hanna looked at Dawn.

"You can join him in death and never see your kids again, or you can do something about your life. But there will be no second chance, Dawn. You fuck this up for yourself, and that will be the end of you as well." It bothered her on so many levels that Dawn had to think if she wanted to live out her life with her children. When she finally nodded that she'd do as she was told, Hanna knew that in a few months, less more than likely, she'd be here again, making sure that Dawn was punished with the same fate as her mate.

After Dawn was taken away, Hanna sat down on the bare ground. Christ, it was exhausting being in charge, and she wondered about what Loren was doing. She hoped that his day was much better than hers was. Or not. They needed to make a stand against the things that most shifter groups were doing.

Chapter 4

Displaying the artwork that the kids did made them feel proud, and it gave him something cheerful to look at. Jeremiah was putting the last of the paintings on the wall board when his room door opened up. He turned his back to the principal and asked him what he wanted. They'd had a huge falling out this morning, and he wasn't in the mood to screw around with him today.

"You're hanging their paintings up, Jerry?" He told him that his name was Jeremiah. "I know what your name is, damn it. I'm making an effort here to be nice. I think that the least you could do was to turn around and look at me when I'm speaking to you."

"Do you have anything more to say than you did this morning?" He finally turned around and regarded the man who had only been working here for two years to his fifteen. "Because the way you treat me now had better be a lot different than the way you spoke to me this morning."

"Are you threatening me, Jerry?" Turning his back on the man again, he reached out for his family, asking if anyone was close to the school. Smiling when his sisters, all four of them, said they were near made him happy. "Because if you are, I'm going to follow through on my threat and have you terminated. What grown man teaches little kids the way that you have for the last ten or twelve years. No one, that's who. You should be the principal like I am. Not some snot nose cleaner for babies."

"I was offered the job of principal here, but I turned it down." The first person to enter the room was Hanna. She simply shoved Cory Laker out of her way and sat down in one of the twenty-three seats that were in his room. Jeremiah wasn't sure if that was good or bad to have her here. She was scarier to him than the others were. "I love teaching, so I didn't take the job. I think I'm good at it, too."

"Sure, I've heard that too. How you've been teacher of the year for the last ten years. Big deal. Did it get you any more money? No? Well, then, it's a stupid thing to win if you ask me." Hanna said that no one had asked him, while both Caitlynne and

Cody came into the room and took a seat, too. "What the hell is this? Who are these women?"

"My sisters. They came to help me pack up my room." He'd not told them that was why he needed them because it hadn't occurred to him until that moment that was what he was going to do. "This is my last day. And as I have paid into my having my summer pay, you'll need to get with the board and have them pay me for that as well."

"You're quitting without notice. I don't have to do shit for you." Caitlynne stood up but sat back down when he stopped her from moving toward Cory. "What was she going to do? Hurt me? I've been around a while, kid. Those women don't scare me. Who are you going to call in now, mommy? Will she help you wipe the noses of these brats that you so love teaching?"

"Let me have at him, please?" Jeremiah shook his head at Cody, not taking his eyes off Cory. "You have to know that he's going to be in trouble if you quit. Let me take him on. I promise you I won't touch him." Caitlynne said she wasn't going to promise that.

"You have to have little sisters help you with your big bad boss." Hanna snorted and drew the attention of Cory. "What? Do you have something to say to me? If so, say it, then get out of here. You're on county property without permission, and I won't stand for it."

When Hanna stood up, the other two women sat down. All she did was move across the room to sit on the edge of his desk. Jeremiah was nervous. Not for himself but what she'd do to Cory. He knew that she'd had a really shitty day yesterday, and this more than likely wasn't helping.

"Do you know the board of the schools around here, Cory?" He told her nope. "I do. As a matter of fact, Jeremiah is on the board. With a lot of other people that live and work around here. I don't know that they'd be all that thrilled to hear the way that you speak to one of their best teachers."

"Best at what? Do they know that he's a grown man teaching these kids?" Hanna asked him if he was jealous. "Of him? Christ no. I became a principal so I'd not have to deal with kids all day long."

"But you're their principal? Doesn't that, I don't know, make you in charge of all the kids that go here? I mean, that's what I would assume, wouldn't you, Jeremiah?" He told her what Cory did all day long while the kids were in the building. "You hide out in your office? Not setting a very good example, are you? Not to mention, I think we pay you to be out there and about with the kids. And taking a five-hour lunch isn't what we, as another board member, pay you for either."

"What are you going to do? Tell on me? They know that I have my hand out to a lot of the businesses around here for charitable donations. It does the school a lot of good to have the community donating a lot of things." Hanna agreed with him and then pointed out that it would help a good deal more if they were to *receive* all the things that they donated. "So? I take a couple of the gift cards. I do spend my own gas money to do this for the school. And who cares if I take a little bit off the top. As I said, I'm doing this on my own dime. No big deal."

"Oh, but it is. You see, I've been keeping track of the 'little bit you take off the top.' Mr. Timler, you spoke to him just this morning about a donation for the Washington, DC, trip the kids are taking. He informed you that he was no longer going to give anything to the school so long as you were here. I believe if you were to go around to any other business, other than the six that you've struck up a deal with, you'll find that same answer. You do know that it's against the law to receive money for tax write-offs, don't you? You also can't write a receipt for double the amount that the person is giving, so they can use it for tax purposes, either. That is about as illegal as anything else that you've done with the school as a cover-up for you."

"Again, are you going to tell on me?" Jeremiah leaned against the chalkboard when he noticed something that apparently Cory had not. There were news crews behind the man. Several of them from the larger cities that were around Ohio. And they were all pointing their phones at him to get the latest scoops. "I'm sure that you'd do the same thing. I know that pretty boy here wouldn't. He's just too nice. Christ, when I think about how the women drool all over themselves when he's on bus duty, it makes me sick. That's the main reason that I've taken that away from him."

"So not only are you a crook, but you're a jealous man too." Hanna laughed a little. "It's a real shame that you couldn't have done a better job for the kids here. I'm sure you might have been able to get a vote or two yourself when it came time to pick out their favorite teacher. Oh, before I forget to tell you. You're fired." Cory laughed.

"You can't fire me. I'm the principal." Hanna laughed and asked Cory what that had to do with anything. "Because you have absolutely no idea how many people I have in my pockets. That beautiful home you have. All the money that the Tates are reported to having? It can be easily taken from you should you try whatever it is you're thinking of doing."

"Did you just threaten the Tate Foundation? Or were you just threatening the people that are Tates? Either way, that's not going to go over very well around here. And how do you think that will work anyway? It won't, in the event that you're going to say something." She looked at the other two women who had come in with her when Shade joined them, too. The four of them could have passed for models. Their beauty surpassed anything he'd ever seen. But it was their power that should have scared Cory a good deal more than it looked like it was.

"Just look at you four. Women all dressed up to do some shopping, I bet. Why don't you just leave here now before I have a talk with some of the charities that you deal with? What do you think they'll say if I were to tell them that you are all four getting a little on the si—"

Jeremiah didn't hesitate for one nano of a second. He just moved. Letting his wolf take him as he lunged at Cory. Just as he took the older man to the floor, he had three thoughts in his head that occurred to him as he was digging his paw into the man's chest.

One. He didn't have a mate, so he was going to be naked when he shifted back. That didn't bother him that much until he thought of number two. He'd be naked in front of his sisters, and that didn't set well with him. It was right then that it occurred to him that there were news crews there, too, and he was going to be naked in front of his sisters. That made him think of one more thing. His brothers were going to murder him.

~*~

Loren laughed every time he looked at Jeremiah. He was livid with himself. Not only that, but the police had put him in cuffs when he shifted back to himself, and he was currently sitting in his class room, buck naked on the floor with a very large towel over his lap that had been in his room too.

"Keep it up, and when I'm lose from here, I'm going to tear you apart." He also noticed that while Jeremiah had a good sense of humor most of the time, today wasn't one of them. For whatever reason, that made him laugh harder. "I'm going to wring your neck, Loren. See that I don't."

"Will you get dressed first? The thought of you trying to strangle Loren with your dick hanging out is just too much for me today." That was another thing that he'd noticed today. Joel had a dirty mind. "It'll be all wiggling around like a loose hose with the water spraying all over the place. You know what I mean, don't you, Layton? That would be just too… wiggly."

"Shut the fuck up." Loren had to go outside and lay on the ground. It had been like this for the last hour. Jeremiah could have been released about three minutes after the police had arrived, but they were having a good laugh with them as well.

"Are you done having fun at your brother's expense?" He shook his head at Hanna. "Well, you've had your fun. Now, go out to his car and get his clothing. He's only asked you to do that about a dozen times now. Besides, I have plans for your body later, and if you're beaten up by your baby brother, you'll suffer too much."

"Why didn't you tell me that sooner?" Loren stood up and kissed Hanna on the mouth. "I love you, my dear. More than I think anyone loves their mate."

He did manage to get clothing for his brother in good time. Handing it off to him, he was happy to see that he'd been released from the cuffs, and it seemed that everyone was finished talking to him about what had happened. Loren told him how sorry he was that he'd made fun of him.

"I guess I would have done the same to you had it been you in here." Pulling on his pants, Jeremiah continued talking to him. "I had no idea that Hanna and the others had planned this out about Cory. How long have they known what he was up to?"

"I don't think all that long. They were talking about it this morning that they had to get to the school before the donations needed to be collected for the fall festival. Shade had found a little bit of it out from one of her patients at the hospital. He was telling her that the donations were much lower last year, and they'd not made as much as they had hoped. After getting a little bit of information, it was Caitlynne who got a lot of it. But since Hanna was willing to confront Laker, Cody got the news crews here to witness it. By the way. What were you needing the women here for in the first place? I think they had planned to do this at his home, but you called for them to help."

"This morning, when I got here, there were several women in the lobby wanting to speak to him. He's never around when there is trouble, and today was no different. He usually shows up after classes begin, only to leave when it's about lunchtime. I was helping them the best I could, just answering questions about the upcoming can drive as well as the after-school program that Caitlynne is working on. Anyway, he finally came to work, and he started telling them that I was wrong about the drive. There wasn't going to be a contest for the rooms with the most as my class usually wins that. And he told them that the after-school program hadn't been approved as yet. I knew that it had, Cody told me just this morning. Well, he got pissy with me, and I walked away from him. I guess he didn't care for that and told the women that I wasn't a team player or something like that. It got back to me. Then, after school was let out, he came back to my room to start on me again. No biggie, I know, but I wanted witnesses to whatever he said to me."

"Hanna told me that Laker has stolen about fifteen grand in donations from the school just this year. Once she started looking into his time off from the school, she told me that he was only spending about three and a half hours at work when he's being paid for fifty. That is money that could have been used for projects at the school if he'd not taken the job." Jeremiah told him that he didn't think it would have been that many hours. "Yes, me too. Every time I go to the diner to pick things up for lunch for us, he's in there. Also, we found out that he wasn't paying for his food there either but charging it off to the school as a facility meeting."

"Damn." Loren fixed his brother's tie, knowing that he would be upset with himself if it wasn't perfect. "I have to talk to the news reporters. I'm glad that they didn't turn me in for being a wolf, but they want to talk to me about what happened here today."

"It's going to be all right, Jeremiah." He still didn't move to go outside to talk to them. "What? You're not nervous, are you? I'll be there with you."

"No, not nervous." He looked at him and then at the door that would take him to the meeting. "I'm going to take the job as principal. I need to make sure that the kids, not just my classroom, are getting everything that they need in the way of funding. Also, I think that I can improve a few things that had been going to the wayside."

"Like the playground." He nodded and said that and other things. "You know that the foundation will help out. And if you need me to be there, I will help out as well."

"I was hoping you'd say that. I'm going to need a lot of help with this, Loren. I have plans." There was no doubt in his mind that he'd follow through on each and every one of them, too. "Thanks. Thanks for being the best big brother."

"You are by and far the best little brother too." The two of them hugged, and true to his word, he followed Jeremiah out into the afternoon sun. There was going to be hell to pay by Cory Laker, and he knew that if anyone could handle it, it would be Jeremiah. Of the six of them, he thought that Jeremiah was the strongest in dealing with things than any of them were.

The news people started to bombard them with questions, but all his brother did was lift his hand, and they quieted down. It was the greatest testament to what he'd been thinking about his brother. He could command the way things went at times.

It took Jeremiah about an hour to tell the crews what had happened in the school today. His attention to detail had them eating up what he was saying from the beginning. When he was finished, he asked if there were any questions, and Loren wasn't surprised to hear the first one was about him being the principal now.

"I've given it a great deal of thought since finding out the schemes that Laker was supposedly doing to the school funding. And I've decided that if the school board will have me, I'll finish out this year for them. That's the best I can offer them because I don't know how I'll do at running the ship when I've only been a crew member for the last few years." The man who had asked the question said that he had his vote. "Thank you for that. It's been a pleasure teaching your son, Hal. He's a good boy."

Most of the others told him that they'd vote for him, too. Not that it was an option. The board would do that on their own. But since two of their sisters and their dad were on the board, it was a shoo-in that he'd get the job. And he'd do a good job of it, too. Of that, there was little doubt.

After things were settled up around the meetings and the school, Loren stayed later to help Jeremiah with the rest of his room. He didn't say all that much, but then, he'd never been a big talker. But when he had something to say, he would listen to him. Finally, when he turned to him after Loren had cleaned off the desks for him, Loren was set to listen.

"You need to come and teach here at the school. High schoolers could learn a few life skills from all of us but you especially." He asked him why he'd think that. "You've done more and seen more than the rest of us. Serving overseas for one thing. But you're the only person I know who still writes checks for his bills. Not to mention, I'm betting that you still have the original social security card you got while in high school. Also, and this is more important than anything else, you're a good person with kids. I've seen you interact with the other kids in the family. They love you."

"They love you too." He said not in a family way but that he was forever giving them good advice. "I just tell them my opinion on things. But only when they ask. I don't go around telling them shit that they don't care about. Besides, when they ask me, I feel like they really want an answer to it, so I make sure that I give them as much as they seem to be interested in."

"And that, my big brother, is what makes you a good person to come around and...maybe not teach the kids but be a counselor for them. Someone to take their questions seriously." Jeremiah said he had a story for him. "Two weeks ago, I had one of the kids, a senior this year, come to me and ask me if it was true that he was only going to be able to do menial labor. He'd been told by his school counselor that he wasn't smart enough. He assured me that she said that for him to hold down any kind of well-paying job, he would have needed to start planning earlier for his education. That his attention span wasn't what it would take for him to do anything but one repetitive job. He'd be good at it, she told him, but that's about all he was worth. She actually told him that was all he'd be worth. I spoke to her. She had the nerve to tell me that she had other kids who weren't destined to be anything but garbage truck workers. Not that there is anything wrong with that profession, but this was a straight-A student when he left here. Now, he's only carrying a low C in his classes because of what she said to him."

"Who?" Jeremiah asked him who he was going to tell. "Who was this paragon of wonderful help to the young minds? I want to sic my wife on her. Hell, any of the women in our family." He told him that it wasn't necessary right now. "You're thinking that I could make a difference to these kids when they're not getting any guidance from someone they should be able to."

"Yes." Jeremiah sat down. "Right now, there are fourteen kids at the high school that are flunking out because the school has let them down. They don't need a study partner, Loren. Nor do they need someone to remind them to do their work. They need someone like you to get in their faces and tell them what the world is and what's out there for them to grab hold of. You know, I'm only a teacher because of you. You got into my face. Remember that?"

"I do. You were flunking second grade. Who the hell flunks second grade? Not you, anyway. So I talked to you." Jeremiah said that he'd knocked him around a bit. "Yes, all right. I did that, too. But you needed it. After that, there was no more — you don't want me to knock a bunch of seniors around, do you? I think there might be laws about that."

"No. Though I would like to see you knock a few heads together that are teachers. They're failing at the very core of our children. They need you. Hell, I need you. Knowing that you're there for them will make my job, seeing them first hand better because I know that you won't let them slip through the cracks. And Loren, there are a lot of cracks in the system around here." He said he'd have to talk to Hanna about it. "Good. And if she can come around and talk to the teachers like she did Cory — she never raised her voice. I think that was the scariest thing was how calm and cool she was. Honestly? I felt my own dick hide away from whatever she was going to do to me."

They both laughed. Then, as they began putting all the desks in neat rows, they talked about what he'd be able to do with the kids at the high school. Jeremiah had a lot of great ideas about it. Loren added a few to them as well. His ever-present notepad was going to be filled up by the time he left. As excited as he'd ever been about something, Loren decided that he was going to do it. If for no other reason than he'd get to help kids like he'd been helped when he'd been in high school.

That night, he spoke to not just Hanna but his older brother as well. He didn't have to clear the job with Joel, but he wanted to make sure that he knew that he'd be there for him, too. Hanna was happy that he was going to be doing something for the kids. Then she told him her plan that she'd been working on with the other women in the family.

"I've been setting up a workshop for kids that

want to learn things like accounting. Spreadsheets. Everyday things, too. Not just on the computer but by having to make one that they can fill out when there isn't one handy. How to read and modify a recipe when cooking. Reading a compass, too. A lot of the kids don't know how to read a map. And I think that would be something very important to learn. GPS isn't always a good thing to depend on when you're in the middle of nowhere." Loren agreed with her on that. He told her how it was difficult at times to find an auction or garage sale in the middle of some dead zone. "See? Everyone would be able to use that. If they want to."

"There would have to be some sort of incentive for this to work. I don't mean money or trophies. Just something that would go toward something that they're trying to achieve. A job out there. Perhaps some college credit. I don't know, but I can look into that for them." She thought that the job incentive sounded the best to her. "I would think that it would for a lot of the kids around here. I know, too, that Joel is working on getting seven industries to set up shop around here. That'll make a lot of jobs open for a great many people."

"Seven?" Loren nodded. "It'll work then. I

have all the faith in the world that it will work out."

Loren hadn't realized how many times since he'd met and fallen in love with Hanna that sevens were in his life. The other day, he'd been in a hurry, running late for another meeting, when he looked at his watch. It was seven minutes after seven. After noticing that, he caught every green light on the way there and arrived seven minutes early. There were other times, too, when he found throughout his day that the number seven played a large part in projects that he was working on.

While he wasn't sure that he believed wholly in the number and the things that it did for him, he was leaning toward it being a good luck number for his daily routine. And that, to him, was a good thing. He hated his routine to be messed with at any time. Loren liked things neat and tidy, everything in its place and nothing left on his desk at the end of the day.

Setting his alarm for tomorrow, he was excited to be doing something for the town. Not that his family didn't already do a great deal for the community, but he was going to get to do this on his own. Something that was his and his alone. He was almost too giddy to sleep. But he thought he had the most delicious distraction and relaxant on the planet. He reached for Hanna.

Chapter 5

Loren didn't have an office. He was disappointed about it, but it wasn't a deal breaker. They were setting him up in the cafeteria for the time being. Watching the kids come in and have a seat far from him was a little disheartening, but he realized too that he was an adult and they hadn't had time to get used to him being there. At least, that was what he was telling himself when he sat there all alone. It was his second day on the job, and he hadn't spoken to a single person. Loren was surprised and nervous when his brother Joel reached out to him.

"Are you currently sitting in the lunchroom at the high school?" He said that he was. Why was he asking? "Nothing bad, not like you're more than likely thinking, but you do have a problem. There is a boy there, a wolf that would love to talk to you. He contacted me because...well, I'm not entirely sure. Hang on."

Loren knew which kids were pack members and who were other shifters. What he didn't know was why they were contacting his brother instead of coming to talk to him. He was right there. When Joel got back to him, he could almost taste the anger in his voice. It was coming through their connection like they were seated next to each other.

"They're not allowed to speak to you." Before he could ask him why not, Joel continued. "The guidance counselor, Mabel Holt, told them that if they were to have any kind of contact with you, either home or here, she would make sure that they got an after-school suspension that would last their entire year."

"Did she say why?" Joel told him. His anger getting so strong that he asked him twice to take a deep breath so that he could talk to him. "So she doesn't want me here and is hoping when she doesn't allow the kids to talk to me that I'll get bored and quit. She doesn't know me all that well, then, is all I can say. I don't give up that easily."

"That's what I told Teddy. He's in the green shirt." Loren said he could see him. "I don't care what you do about this. But I would very much like it if you did something. And when she does try and suspend the kids, Dad told me that he'll be there first thing to take care of her. Can't fire her without a valid excuse. To me, we have one, but I'm not the one in charge. And so you know, I've not told the women. I don't want to have to bail them out if it…what am I talking about, not if it gets out of hand but when it does. This isn't right."

"I'll take care of it here if you're sure that Dad can make it so that they're not in trouble. I want to make this work not just for me but especially for them." He thought of Mabel. "Joel, do you remember her from when we were kids? How she used to tell us that we'd never amount to anything because we had money? I thought for sure that Mom set her straight on a couple of those issues that she had with us. Apparently not. I'm thinking that she needs to be gone."

"I agree. I'm with Dad now. I'm going to tell him what I know, and you do whatever you need to do to get the kids talking to you. I don't know why we didn't think of this before. Loren, I think this, you being there for them, will be a good thing for a great many of those kids." He thanked him. "No need for that. I'm going to talk to Jeremiah, too. This was brilliant. But only if we can get to them. All right? You need anything from me?"

"Not right now. But you might need to be close if this gets bad. And I have no idea why, but I think it will have to get bad before it gets fixed." Joel agreed. "Thank you for giving me a heads up. I'll take care of it here."

After thanking Joel again, he closed their connection. Getting up, he went to the table where the kids were hanging out and sat down with them. They looked about as nervous as he was when an adult would come around while in school. He just needed something to break the ice.

"Did you know that you can turn your phone on so that it has a compass? I use it all the time." Taking out his phone, he decided that he was going to be dumb a little here. "I know that there are several apps that you can use. It's just figuring out which one to use. Do you guys use an app that I can figure out?"

None of them moved when he asked. After a few tense moments, Teddy took his phone from him and showed him which one his grandda used. They used it when they went hunting, he said. After a few mistakes in getting the phone set up, two more of the boys joined in the conversation.

He'd never thought of using a compass to find his way around his own yard. But Teddy had told the others that he used it all the time when he wanted to hide out in the trees at their home. After figuring out in which direction he went, it was simple for him to get back home without taking too many twists and turns. The six of them talked about the idea of hanging out in the trees when they were looking for a way to get out of chores.

"What are you doing here, Mr. Tate? I thought you were an accountant or something for your family business." He explained that he was there to help them out with questions they might have. "Like what? You mean about how to save money? You gotta have some before you can save it at my house."

And that started them out in talking about what kind of jobs they wanted to get when they were out of school. Loren was in his element and having a good time. When the bell rang for lunch period to begin for the next group, he was still sitting there when a bunch of other kids joined in on the talk. Word must have traveled fast because by the time lunch was over for the school, he'd spoken to thirty kids and had three pages of notes.

As he was cleaning up the mess he'd made with his own lunch, Mrs. Holt came out of the main offices. She didn't sit down but stood over him. When she began to speak at him, not to him, Loren stood up. He towered over her. She backed away from him, but he could tell that she was pissed.

"What do you think you're doing?" he said he was doing his job. "You're making these kids have big dreams when there is nothing that will come out of it."

"Why don't you want them to dream big? I would think that it was something all teachers aspire to. The kids they teach to have big dreams." She said she wasn't a teacher. "So. You're still supposed to be there for them. Helping them manage school and getting into college, aren't you?"

"None of the kids you were speaking to have any ambition. They're not going anywhere but in the unemployment line or the welfare office to get assistance. When teachers build them up, it's me that has to bring them back to reality. And I'm sick of it. Sick to death of having to be the one who tells them that they're going nowhere at all. It's what's wrong with this town. People don't want to go to work. Look at you. You, with all your money, isn't helping them at all. They see you here spouting off big ideas that you have, and they have to go home to their drunk or high parents. They'll be like all the rest. Dead beats and drunks." He had to sit down. Loren couldn't believe what was spilling from her mouth. "You want to help them? Then, stay away from them. You telling them big stories of college and well-paying jobs isn't going to help them. Not one of them are going to go to college. They're lazy and stupid. All of them are. Christ, I wish I had a nickel for every kid that came through my office wanting an application to college, and I have to tell them they can't have one. They're stupid. Too stupid to even be alive if you ask me. They certainly shouldn't be breeding. There are enough of their kind around here now; they don't need to be making more of them. And that's what they'll do, too. Breed more of their kind until we're a town of inbreeds."

"My god. Why are you even here? You're a bitter old bitch that shouldn't be near children at all. Christ, when I think of the way the kids were excited to have someone listening to them, I understand why now. You aren't there. Not for them. Not for the community. You should be fired." She said they knew better than to mess with her. She had it all worked out. "I'm going to the board about you. You're off your rocker if you think that after everything you just said to me that no one is going to look into you."

"You think I care? Your mother. That's what this is all about, isn't it? That your lovely sainted mother couldn't get me fired, so you think that you will. Well, you're not. You're just as stupid as she was if you want to know the truth." Loren stood up. He could take her yelling at him, but she wasn't going to get by with talking about his mom that way. "Look at you. All big and strong. What are you going to do, Loren. Knock me around? Beat me up? Or are you going to turn into that monster of yours and rip my throat out? Go ahead and try. I dare you."

He had it in his head to do just what she had said. To rip her throat out. But he picked up his phone off the table where he'd been talking to the kids and dialed first the police, then he called his brother. It was then that he noticed that his phone had been set on record. Looking to where the kids had gone, he saw Teddy standing there with his phone out and the principal standing next to him.

Mr. Gray had his mouth hanging open. As if he couldn't believe the things that he'd heard either. Once he had his brother on the line, he felt sick to his stomach. Holding his belly when he explained to Joel what was going on, he nearly shifted when the sound of a gun went off right beside him.

~*~

Hanna continued to hold Loren's hand. He'd not spoken a word since he'd handed his phone over to the police when they arrived. Joel had gone to their home to get him some clean clothing, but the ambulance that had arrived too had him change into scrubs so that the police could take his clothing. It was evidence for them.

"Is Teddy going to be all right?" He'd asked her that four times now, and each time, she told him that he was at the hospital. Hanna didn't tell him that he had died too, but she thought that he understood that part but wasn't ready to think about it. "Without him, I wouldn't have known any of this. I want to make a fund for a scholarship in his name. Without him, none of this would have come out."

"All right. I think that Joel said that they'd do it through the foundation." Loren told her that he wanted to do it, too. For the rest of them. "All right, love. We'll talk about it when we get to go home. Are you ready to leave yet?"

"I don't know." He looked at her. His eyes

didn't seem to be as glazed over as they had been when she'd gotten here. "She killed them. Mr. Gray, Teddy. Nearly me, too, didn't she?"

"Yes. She was sick." He nodded and then looked in the direction where the two bodies were of Teddy and the principal. "Honey, don't look. Okay? Just talk to me. You're scaring me a bit. Just talk to me."

"You said she was sick. She was out of her mind. You should have heard what she was saying to me. It was all things that...what would make her think that anyone would be all right with anything that she was doing? How did she get away with it for so long?" Hanna told him that the police were looking into things. "They'll have to dig really deep, Hanna. I think she's been like this... She talked about my mom, too. Like she held a grudge against her or something. My mom was a sweetheart."

"That's what I heard too." He looked at her, and she could see that his eyes, like most of the people here right now, were filled with tears. "She's gone now. I wish that someone had been able to get to her sooner. So many lives are ruined because of her. And today, she took the lives of two people that no more deserved to die than she did having this job."

Loren pulled her to him, and he held her tightly. She could feel his body shaking with the tears he was shedding. She could feel his anger, too. Such senseless murders. Teddy and Mike had lost their lives because they'd been in the wrong place at the wrong time. And if the security officer that had just come on duty hadn't of been armed, too, there might well have been a lot more lives taken.

It was nearly six-thirty when they said that they could go home. She was ready for it, too. Her need to pamper Loren, to hold him tightly, was overwhelming for her. Even when they got to the parking lot, and Joel was there, she wanted to tell him to leave Loren alone that she had it. But she stopped when Jeremiah told her how sorry he was.

"Sorry for what?" He said that he'd asked Loren to go there. "Thank you for that. There is no telling how much worse this might have been—"

"But she killed those people. It's my fault." She didn't hesitate but slapped him across the face. "That's not helping."

"Why do you think this is your fault? Did you arm her? Did you—did anyone tell you what was in her office when they searched it, Jeremiah? That she had a list of things to do today that included not just killing the staff here but to kill all of the senior class? That their names were listened in order of stupidity, she called it." He said that he'd not known that. "I'm sure you didn't. Or you'd not be spouting off to me and your brother how this was all your fault. If he'd not been there. If he'd not distracted her enough that she didn't get to the list, a great many more deaths would have — she tried to kill him. She tried to kill my Loren, and there you stand telling me that it's your fault."

"I'm so sorry, Hanna." The two of them sobbed great tears together. She held him tightly as he pulled his brother into the hug. "I didn't even know that she worked here anymore. But when I heard that…what she'd done, it was all I could do not to — I thought that you'd both blame me for asking Loren to be there."

"It's good that he was. Without him there, as I said, she might well have been able to kill off a lot of good kids. The police said that Loren had distracted her from her plan. She'd been watching him on closed circuit television and had left her list behind." She cried harder. "If you would have come here too, she might well have hurt you too. I don't know that I could have stood that, to be honest with you, Jeremiah. My heart is nearly broken now.

If something happened to you, too…Don't say this was your fault to me again. Do you hear me? Never again."

"Yes, ma'am." He laughed a little. "You sometimes remind me of my mom. She was like you. All sloppy upset yet making a point. I love you, Hanna."

"And I love you, you dork. Come home with us. I need to get your brother into the shower and something for him to eat." Jeremiah said that he'd ordered Chinese food just before he'd heard what had happened here. "Yes, the police were keeping things quiet so that the parents didn't come here in mass."

"Jeremiah, will you double your order and come home with us?" Loren hugged his brother. "I'm feeling better now. Not great, but it's not taking his toil on me as much as it…I was standing right next to her when she was killed. My clothing is…I'm going to burn it."

"Good for you. I'll help you." Jeremiah hugged him again. "Just so you know, big brother, the entire town is talking about how you saved the day. So don't be surprised when they thank you. I think that a lot of parents were terrified that something like this was going to happen with her. It scares me to think that she got away with it for so long."

"That's what the police are saying too. I'm sure that there are going to be some people losing their jobs over this." Loren looked at his brother Joel as he talked with the mayor. "Did you hear that Homer, the mayor, is retiring this year? I think this is going to be something that makes his retirement sooner rather than the end of the term. You should take the job, Hanna. You'd be really good at keeping the town on the up and up."

She didn't tell him no because she'd been thinking that his father should take it. However, she did tell Jeremiah to get the food and to meet them at their home. Not that they were celebrating or anything, but Loren had told her just the other day that Chinese food was his go-to food for comfort. Apparently, it was something that his mother enjoyed a great deal.

By the time Loren was getting out of the shower, the food was ready to be picked up. They had invited Joel over with his family because he told them he wanted to talk about some kind of memorial for Teddy and Mike. While Mike had been human, he had tried to shield Teddy when the gun had been pointed at him. There were heroes all around the school that she was hearing about since being home.

"I just got off the phone with Homer. He said that he's going to turn in his paperwork tomorrow. That his heart just can't take any more things like this. He does want to work with the incoming mayor on some of the things that are going on, but he and his missus are going to go away. And he said he wasn't thinking about returning." Hanna told Loren that they should help them with the moving or whatever they needed. "I did. I made sure that they were out of town quietly. Not that I think anyone would blame them for anything that happened at the school, but he said he couldn't take it anymore. I don't blame him."

Loren pulled her into his arms and held her. She wanted to stay this way with him forever but knew that they did have things to talk about. One of them being the things for the pack. However, it was in her mind, too, that there was nothing that was that important that couldn't be put off until tomorrow. Tonight was for family.

Jeremiah showed up about the time that Joel came over. Caitlynne was going to be late as she had gone to talk to Teddy's parents and to help them out.

Teddy had been their only child, so they were taking it especially hard. Not that she could blame them. It would be hard, she thought, if there were fifty children in the family.

"The pack is paying for the funeral. Everything. And pay the family while they're home grieving. I told them to take as long as they needed. I can't imagine what they're feeling right now." Joel hugged his brother three times before he backed away. "This was just too close. I know that we're all immortal, but the thought of one of you guys being shot, well, it tears my heart up something terrible. I don't want anything to happen to any of you guys."

"Same here. When she pointed that gun at my head, all I could think about was that I didn't tell you guys that I love you today. And that I wanted to see Hanna again." Loren started to cry a little and left the room. Jeremiah went out the front door to have a minute, too.

"He blamed himself for this." Joel asked her what she'd done to him to make him see reason. "Slapped him. I might well you too if you give me any shit about it."

"Never. And sometimes, as my grandda used to say, you have to slap some sense into someone before they'll listen." Joel sat down at the table, helping her put the large white boxes around it. "They found her husband. Thomas Holt had been killed earlier this morning. The police told me that he was sitting at the kitchen table where his coffee cup was still in his fingers when she'd done it. They're assuming that she'd done it, but they're not saying anything right now. She had all kinds of notes at her home, too, that talked about how she was the only smart one in the county. How it was going to be left up to her to keep the stupid people from having more stupid people. They're calling their children in now. I didn't even know she had a husband, much less two kids. Finding the phone numbers for them was easy. She had laid it out with her will and her medication before leaving for work this morning. Whatever didn't happen today, I think that we were very lucky that Loren was there."

"That's all. Okay? I don't want to talk about anything that has to do with the school until later. We dodged a bullet, and I, for one, will be ever so grateful to the police and the others for keeping it as low-key as they could for the parents." She sat down. "One more thing, then I'm going to take my own advice. My heart hurts for Teddy and his family, Joel. We need to make this less tragic and more productive for the town. Loren said that he wants to personally pay for a scholarship for two students. I'm on board with that."

"The foundation will as well." Joel kissed her on the cheek, and she asked him what that was for. "For not falling apart. I did. So did Caitlynne when we were told about the shooting and deaths. You kept us all going forward and not dwelling on the things that we couldn't change. Even Donnie, the first cop on sight, said that you kept him focused on the job and not the blood that was everywhere."

"He told me that he'd never seen so many bodies at one time. That it made him sick. All I did was hand him a peppermint and told him to suck it up. I don't know even now if I meant the peppermint or the job, but he got to work." Joel laughed and said that he'd said the same thing. "Yes, well, I've been around for a bit longer than you have, so I've seen things that I can never unsee. Speaking of which, I saw my dad today. Christ, he's a whiney wiener, isn't he?" Loren laughed as he came into the dining room, taking a plate from her as he passed by.

"What does he want now? I heard him telling Mr. Tillman that he'd never hurt so much as he did now. Tillman, who only has one leg and is blind, told him to get the hell away from him. That he didn't know real pain until you were stuck under your tractor for two days without nary a slice of bread or a banana. Mr. Tillman should be mayor. He'd keep us all in stories, that's for sure."

Jeremiah filled his plate, too, as he was telling them stories of Mr. Tillman. The man sounded like a character, that's for sure. To hear the stories about the man, one would think that he'd won the war all by himself, but he'd never served. Also, his wife, they said, was just as funny.

"Two or three years ago, she entered the pie baking contest. We need to have more things like that again, Joel. A week of things that we used to do when we were kids. Roast a hog. Have some fireworks. That would be great." Hanna asked him about the pie baking contest. "Yeah. She entered it. No one could understand why she'd do that. From what her husband would tell about her, she couldn't cook worth nothing. And baking was something that she was forbidden to do. The judges, as you can imagine, had their trepidation about tasting her pie. It was pretty. Decorated with the extra dough to look like an entire bouquet of flowers were put on it. So when it was time to do the tasting, they had Homer taste it first." Jeremiah started laughing before he could finish.

"I'll finish it for you, dummy." Loren laughed, too, but not nearly as hard as Jeremiah was. "Homer took the smallest bite he could. Just touched it to his tongue while everyone was watching him. People were actually standing by with their phones out in case they needed to call an ambulance or something. Then he smiled. It wasn't a happy smile, but he did it as he dug a deeper bite out of the pie and ate it."

Loren stopped talking then, and she wanted to bash his head in. Finally having enough, she turned to Saul to ask him what had happened. But it was useless. He was already eating, and his mouth was stuffed full of egg roll. It was Joel who finally told her the rest.

"It was terrible. It was…it was just a baked pie. No filling. She'd not heard that they were going to be tasting it. She just thought they were going to be looking for the pretties pie. And she did have that. But it was nothing but crust through and through. Dry crust, too, that a person could barely bite into. They gave her a ribbon for her best-looking pie. If I remember correctly, she stuck it to her fridge and never baked again."

"Oh, I love that woman." They had stories about a lot of people in town that she enjoyed. It was the perfect thing to do when there had been so much tragedy earlier. When they were finished up eating, they all went out on the back deck and told more stories. Not just of the townspeople but of their family, too. Hanna enjoyed every moment of it.

When Caitlynne arrived, much later than anyone expected, she told them what had happened. Teddy's parents were grief-stricken and barely able to function. But food was coming to the house.

"I had a couple of the ladies from the pack stay there to get things squared away for them. Jacob's brother took things to the funeral home for them. And Charlie, Teddy's grandda, was making the arrangements. He looks ten years older than the last time I saw him." Joel held Caitlynne as she spoke. "They're going to have the funeral at the high school. I think that the plan is to have them at the same time. Charlie said that he didn't think that the funeral home was going to be big enough. Everyone knew and loved his grandson, and they'd want to pay their respects to the family. I agreed with him."

"We'll do whatever they need." Caitlynne said

that she'd told them that as well. "Shade is coming over later. She said that she can work a little magic for them so that neither of them will look as if they'd been shot." Joel was taking it hard as well, she could see.

The rest of the family came by a few at a time. They were there to find out if they could do anything for anyone. All of them hugged their brother. Loren was doing much better now that he was out of the clothing that they'd had him wear. Not to mention the blood off himself.

Hanna knew that for as long as she lived, this would be something that would haunt her. Not that she was there, nor did she see what happened when it went down. But it was something that she'd think about every time she passed the school or dropped off her own children there. She didn't think that having a kind of memorial plaque would help, but they would need to do something to make the memory of it less painful. She'd give it some thought. Perhaps even get with the rest of the family to make it happen.

That night, when she went to bed, she held Loren tighter to her. Every time he moved, even to roll over, she sat up in the bed to make sure he was all right. She wondered if she would ever get over the feelings of nearly losing him. Not that she would have, she had to keep reminding herself, but it was just too fresh for her to let it go right now. She'd be all right, she knew. As soon as she got over the feeling of complete helplessness like she'd had when she heard that there had been a shooting at the high school.

Chapter 6

"Hello." Chalina wasn't in the mood today to deal with people. Not that she was normally, but most days, she could hide it well enough that people didn't stare at her when she snapped. But today wasn't going to be an easy day. "I said Hello. Is there anyone there?"

"Yes. Sorry. My name is Loren Tate. I'm in a small town in Ohio. Is this Chalina Holt?" She said that she was. "I'm trying to reach a Chad Holt. I'm to understand that you are his wife."

"Ex-wife. I've no idea where he is. Try prison." Loren told her that he had information about his parents. "I'm sure that he won't care one bit. But what happened to Clarence? Did the old bitch finally kill him off? She threatened to do that to me on more than one occasion."

The little boy that came into the doctor's office waiting room where she was waiting sat across from her. Like there weren't seven hundred seats all around the fucking room. Stretching her neck, she heard and felt a good pop from it and was glad to see that the boy's eyes widened in shock. He started shaking his mom, who had the 'let me see your manager' hairstyle along with her phone stuck so close to her face it wouldn't have surprised her if she couldn't see the entire screen. Loren started talking, and she realized she missed something.

"I'm sorry. I've had a bad week, Mr. Tate. I've broken my ankle five days ago, and I've been barely getting around. My daughter has been—I'm sorry. Like you care about my woes. I don't know where Chad is." He must have said it once already, but he told her that Clarence was indeed dead, and so was Mable. She had killed him. "Christ. She's the most bigoted woman I've ever met. Her son isn't that much different. Did you say she was dead, too?"

"Yes. She shot him in the morning. Or, I should say, allegedly shot him before leaving for work. Once there, she got into an altercation with me and killed a student as well as a member of the facility. The police killed her when she wouldn't drop her gun." She hated that Clarence was gone. She really had loved that old man. The kid came over to where she was and grabbed her knee scooter. Chalina told him to stop that. "Are you all right?"

"Not really. There is this kid that is—what do you want?" The kid told her that he wanted to have her scooter. "No. Can't you see that I'm using it? Not to mention, I need it to get around. Go back to your mother."

"No. I want it, and you're going to give it to me. You're not using it." She told him that she was indeed using it and that he couldn't have it. "But I want it."

When he started pulling it out from under her foot, her broken foot, it was all she could do not to cry when he continued to bump her tender leg. When he started screaming for his mother, she finally pulled her phone out of her face.

"Lady, control your kid before I hurt him." Of course, that set Manager Mom off, and she told him that he was a good kid. "It's really telling when you have to tell someone that right off the bat that he's good. When obviously, he isn't anywhere close to that. Tell him to leave my scooter alone. It's mine."

"Oh, don't be so selfish. Just let him have it. It's

not like you're using it. I don't want to have to deal with it right now. I'm talking to someone." Chalina told the kid again to back off, or she was going to take matters into her own hands. "You're not going to touch my child. He's just wanting to play with that thing. Just be nice and let him have it."

"Oh, I'm going to let him have it all right. Either you make him stop, or I'm going to give it to him, but good. Damn it, woman, he's fucking hurting me." She remembered that she was on the phone when she heard Loren laughing. "I'm going to have to call you back. I have a situation here that I'm not going to come out on top with."

Closing the connection, she put her phone down, grabbed the handle of the scooter and let the kid have just enough of it so that he thought that he had won. When he smiled at her, a smile of 'fuck you' if she'd ever seen one, she pushed the scooter as hard as she could right into his chest. Not only did he go tumbling ass over head, but he hit his mom's phone and sent it flying. The nurse came out to call her name just as she was setting her scooter upright again.

"She tried to hurt my son. I want you to call the police." The nurse just looked at her and winked.

Then she reminded the woman, Ms. Pillar, that there were cameras in the room and the police knew from the last time that her son was the culprit. "I don't understand why no one will just give him what he wants. It works for me at home, and I don't have any trouble with him at all. Christ. You people need to take a pill or something. He's a good boy." Chalina put her knee on the scooter, leaving her foot dangling painfully off the end of it. She turned to the mother.

"Yeah, I just bet he is when he is forever getting his way. What do you suppose is going to happen when you finally have to tell him no? I'm sure that will go very just fine and dandy." She made her way into the office, nearly sick with the pain in her foot.

Once she was in one of the many rooms, the nurse came in a few minutes later with a shot for the pain. She'd never been so grateful for something in her life than right then. As she was letting the medication roll over her, she thought of her daughter and what she'd say when she told her what she'd done today.

Chalina wasn't in as much pain when Lynn got home. Of course, she'd had her foot up for about an hour now, and most of the swelling had gone down. Letting Lynn fuss over her for a few minutes, she finally got her to settle down and talk to her. Asking her about her school got the same reaction she would have gotten if she'd asked her if she'd have greens for dinner. A look that had her laughing.

"Mom, have you seen the papers that I saved for you? It talks about father's family." She told her that she'd not seen them yet and that she'd gotten a call from someone there today. "It says that Grandma Holt killed three people, one of them being Grandpa Clarence. She was set to kill the entire school off before she went home that day. I guess something else happened, and she was only able to—not that two more people isn't a lot, but she didn't kill the ninety-four seniors that were on her list. She was forever making lists about things that you did, huh?"

"Yes, most of them were all in her head." She was given the last week of papers. Reading the headlines, she told Lynn that it was Loren Tate who had called her. "He was trying to get in touch with your father. I don't suppose you've heard from him, have you?"

"The day you fell. He called to tell me that he wasn't going to be able to pick me up this weekend that something had come up. Like I was surprised by that. Anyway, I told him how you'd broken your ankle, and he didn't seem to care. Not that I thought he would." This would be the tenth weekend in a row that Chad hadn't picked up his daughter for the weekend. She asked her if she was all right with that. "Yes. I hate going there anyway. His new girlfriend is a nasty sort of person. She's really a bitch, but you won't let me say that."

"And yet you did." Tickling Lynn, she had her laughing before she told her that she needed to give the number to Mr. Tate. "Chad needs to know that his parents are gone. It would be terrible for him to find out too late to make it to their funeral."

"Do you think that he'd go?" Chalina thought that the only way that he'd go was if he had someone take him there, set up the arrangements for him and make sure that he got to the funeral home on time. But she didn't say that to her daughter. She more than likely knew it, but Chalina tried very hard not to talk badly about Chad to his child. "I'll call him. But you have to order something for us to eat. I'm sick of canned soup."

When Lynn went to her room to call her dad, Chalina laid back on the couch. Thinking about the Holts now, she wondered what people would say if she told them that she knew that this day was coming.

Mable was just one short hot fuse away from having the kind of meltdown that she'd had at the school. She remembered the first time that she'd met the woman.

"Who do you think you are being around my son? You're not good enough." Chalina had stood up, perfectly happy with the fact that someone else agreed with her about not marrying Chad. "Where the heck are you going? I'm not finished telling you how you're not good enough for the Holt name."

"I'm perfectly happy with not being a Holt. If your bastard of a son hadn't drugged me and raped me, then—" The slap to her face was so surprising and painful that Chalina had punched back. Not only did she knock the woman over, but she had busted her lip too. "You will never hit me again. Do you understand me?"

"You're a cunt." Chalina didn't even bother denying it. Then Mable turned to her son. "Why did you bring this slut to my home? You had to know that I wouldn't approve."

"She's going to have my son." Even then, in the first couple of months of her pregnancy, Chalina knew that she was not going to have a boy. It scared her still what they might have done to her to have her leaving a son behind. And there was no doubt in her mind that they would have harmed her. They were terrible to her the few weeks after Lynn had been born. A divorce from Chad was easy to get because she'd been told that there would be no more children of her body.

Gary Sloan had promised her that Chad would never find out that it had been a lie. That she could have had a hundred children and never had any trouble. But since it had come from a doctor, a male doctor, Chad signed the divorce papers that afternoon, and she'd been free of him since. And even though they did share a daughter, he rarely, if ever, spoke to her directly. Which was fine by her.

"He wants to talk to you." Lynn stood in front of her with her phone out. "Mom? Dad said that he wants to talk to you about the shooting. I don't think that he believes me."

She took the phone and waited for a few seconds to listen to what Bitch, she hadn't any idea what his new girlfriend's name was finished talking. That was a huge pet peeve of hers. When you want to talk to someone, then do it. When Chad finally said her name, she asked him what he wanted.

"Daughter said that my parents are dead. Is

this some kind of joke for you? You know that my mother is a god-fearing woman. She'd never kill anyone." Chalina said that it was in the papers that she not only killed her husband, but she killed a seventeen-year-old as well as a member of the faculty at the school where she worked. "Why would she do something like that? Someone provoked her. What did you do to her?"

"Me? I've not spoken to your mother in nine years, Chad. Your father told me the last time I spoke to him, which was about a month ago, that she was making lists again about the bad people where she worked. Other than that, I haven't any idea." Chad asked if she was going to the funeral. "I will take Lynn if she wants to go."

"I'll take her." She didn't bother telling him that he wouldn't take her anywhere but let him think that he was still making decisions for her. "You have her ready, and I'll make arrangements to have her picked up by someone."

"No." She knew that he hated that word more than he did anything else. "No one I don't know is going to be taking Lynn anywhere that I'm not there too. And we'll only go if that's what Lynn wants to do. Otherwise, you're to stay away from me, or I will have the police involved. I've told you this before, Chad: I have a restraining order against you for you to stay fifty feet from me at all times."

"You're stupid. Mother always told me that, too. I shouldn't have married you." Chalina said that she wished he'd not either. "Good. Then we can agree on one thing. I'm going to check into things. If you're lying to me, so help me, Chalina, I will break the law to break your fucking scrawny neck."

Putting the phone on the coffee table as gently as she could, she looked at Lynn when she asked her if she was all right. Nodding then shaking her head, Lynn came to the couch, careful of her foot and hugged her. It was the best medicine she'd ever get, she thought.

"I did want to go, but I don't think that is a good idea. I loved Grandpa Holt. Not so much Grandma Holt, but he was always so good to me." Chalina said that they'd be all right. That she figured that she'd want to say goodbye to him. "I really do. I loved his so much."

They dined on pizza and chocolate milk, talking about her grandparents throughout the night. Mostly, as she thought would happen, it was more about Clarence than Mable. Mable had never liked her, and she treated Lynn like she was some kind of insect in a lab. Chalina wasn't even sure that the elderly woman had ever once held Lynn when she'd been a child, nor hugged her when she got older. It was her loss, she thought.

It was nearly nine when she remembered she'd not called Loren back. Thinking that it was much too late, she messaged him instead. Asking him if he'd call her when it was convenient for him. Two minutes later, her cell phone rang.

"I'm so sorry it's so late. I had my daughter call Chad. He's supposed to be calling to find out if she's really gone." Loren laughed and said that he'd heard from the man and that he didn't think that he would be calling him again. "That bad, huh. I should have warned you about Chad. He's not the sharpest tool in the box. Worse yet, he's just like his mother. And if you say that to him, he'll act like you've given him some kind of award about it. They're both terrible people. Clarence was a good man."

"Yes, that's what we've been finding out. I'm still trying to find her other child. We didn't know that she had any children, and it turns out that she had two. Do you happen to know where James is?" She told him what had happened to James. "I'm so sorry to hear that. Like I said, we didn't know there were any children, and I apologize for bringing it up."

"I didn't know him all that well. I knew that he had a terrible relationship with his mother and brother. There are some who say that Chad drove him to commit suicide. But I don't know for sure. He was a better man, by all accounts, than Chad. Which really wouldn't have to be too much. Chad is a bastard and a prick on his best days." Loren laughed. "I don't have any idea why I find it so easy to talk to you. I guess it could be that I'm starved for adult conversation. Lynn is the only real person I see most days. Until I got hurt."

"Did Chad do that to you?" She wondered how he had figured that out and said nothing to the man. "I see. Well, when you get here, you nor your daughter will have to worry about him. My family will protect you both. I didn't mention this before, but the attorney for your father-in-law said that when I spoke to you again to let you know that you and your daughter are both mentioned in his will. There wasn't one for Mable. I don't know why, but that's what he told me."

"Lynn and I will be there in a couple of days.

If you could set us up someplace, I'd be grateful. I can't put any weight on my foot for another three weeks. So if you can find us someplace low to the ground, I'd appreciate it." He said that he could do that. "Thank you so much, Loren. I'll give you a call when we arrive, and you can tell me where we're staying. I'm assuming that you have a taxi service there? Hopefully?"

He laughed again. "I'm afraid not. But you give me your flight information, and I'll make sure that you're picked up." The man was being much too nice, and she thought for sure that she was simply starved for a little male attention, and that was all it was. "All right, Chalina. You give me a call when you have your flight information, and someone will pick you up at the airport."

After getting off the phone with him, she sat up on the couch. Stripping down to her panties, she pulled her gown over her head and laid back. She thought about going to her bed, but it was just too much effort. Covering up with the blanket that she'd been using since she'd gotten hurt, Chalina closed her eyes and thought about Chad.

He'd never been nice to her. Not even when she told him that she was going to have a baby. It wasn't in her mind to tell him about Lynn, but when he cornered her at work and nearly punched her in the face, she told him to save herself. Fat lot of good it had done her. He still knocked her around when he was close enough to find her.

Crying a little, feeling sorry for herself, Chalina let sleep take her under. Tomorrow was going to be a long day, and she needed to be on her toes in order to get through it. Getting a flight to Ohio was the least of her worries. Trying to keep Chad away from her while there was going to be a lot of hard work. Maybe Loren would be able to protect her. But only while she was there. He'd still come after her when she got back home.

~*~

Loren laid out his notebooks while sitting at the lunchroom table. They did have an office for him, but he'd not wanted to be in it just yet. He supposed he wanted to see if the kids would accept him after all the things that had gone down. If they didn't, he'd just not come back. When one of the students, Jamie, he thought his name was sat down across from him, he asked him if he was staying.

"I was just thinking the same thing. I'm not sure. I didn't know how you guys would react to me being here." They'd had two weeks off from school for the funeral as well as to get the school remolded. His family had helped with that. As well as a good many of the students and parents. Mable's office was now a file room. The walls had been repainted, and new carpet had been laid. Her desk and everything that had been in the room had been put into the dumpster. No one was more happy about that than he was. "How are you guys holding up?"

"All right. Most of us have been going my Teddy's house to help out his mom. His dad, he never talks to any of us. I think he's taking it pretty hard. I know that I probably would, too." Loren told Jamie that it was difficult for a parent to lose a child, but the way that they'd lost Teddy was ten times worse. "That's what my mom and dad told me. Teddy was a good guy. I'm going to miss him. He was a good ball player, too."

Some of the other kids came to join them at the table. They talked about Teddy and Mr. Gray. They all had good memories of the two of them. Loren hadn't known that Mike was Teddy's homeroom teacher until then. He'd been their coach, too.

"Mr. Loren? Do you think it's possible that some of us could get a few applications to college? I know that it's pretty late, but we weren't allowed to ask for them when…well, you know what she said." He nodded and smiled. "We don't even care if it's a college with a football team there. We just really want to go. Well, most of us do."

"As a matter of fact, I've been able to get a lot of information from a great many colleges for you guys. My family put the word out about needing information for you guys to be able to get a late start on college applications. After a few calls — and because everyone had heard about what had been going on here, there are over three dozen college reps coming here on Saturday to help you guys get going on it. A lot of the colleges, too, are sending information directly here so that I can get it to you. They're willing too to waive the application fees and look over your applications right away so you have a fair chance." He pulled out the list of colleges that were coming and handed it around.

"This is great. Wow, Ohio State is going to help us out, too?" Loren told Jamie that they were even going to send out a football rep to check out who they could recruit, too. "This is fantastic. I mean, even if we don't get on the team, it'll be so great to be able to say we were looked at."

The kids were so excited that when the bell rang for them to go to class, he didn't want them to leave. It was obvious that they didn't either. But more kids came to the dining area, and they were just as excited as the first group were. By the end of the day, Loren knew that he'd be back tomorrow and the next day to just have the same feelings he'd gotten today.

Hanna was waiting for him near his car when he left the building. After telling her how his day went, he could see that she was much more relaxed, too. He knew that she'd been worried about him going back to the school, and he loved that he'd been able to make her happy with the results of the day.

"I've been talking to your dad. He said that in a couple of weeks, you guys would be pulling out all the stops for Halloween. I didn't think that grown men liked that holiday." He said that it had been his mom's favorite, and they all enjoyed it because she had. "I can see that. He also told me that you guys have a not so friendly competition on who has the best decorated house too. We're going to win that this year, just so you know."

"I don't know. For the last five years, it's been Dad. He has the best time decorating. I'm betting if you were to go out to the garage, he's already got a lot of the decorations out and sprucing them up. He has a lot of decorations. Blow up stuff, too." She said that she could make things for them as well. "We can't use magic. That's one of the rules. Not that any of us had as much as we did now when we started this, but that was the one thing that Mom wouldn't allow. No magic."

"Well, that sucks. I had all these plans about how I was going to have ghosts there, as well as a few creepy guys. I guess I'll have to go shopping to see what I can find." He told her that there were a lot of things in the barn behind their home. "Really? I would love to, you know we only have about a month to get ready. I hope you're prepared to work really hard after school every day. Who does the voting anyway?"

"The kids that come around. They each get a ticket from each of us with our names on them. Then, they get to put the cauldron in the middle of the square. I don't know who will count them this year, but it used to be Homer doing it." She said that she could maybe find someone that would help count them out. "We should have Aurora do it. I think she'd do it just for the fun of being around the kids. She hands out candy, too, at one of the houses.

The big bars, too. Also, she gives out a little magic to those that she sees needs it. I think she loves doing that around here."

"How sweet of her. I'm assuming that the magic is something tangible that she notices with the families." He told her that it was and asked her if she wanted dinner out. "No. Mrs. Sheppard made us a big pot of soup. I so love this time of year when soup is added to so many menus."

He loved soup, too. Potato cheese was his all-time favorite, with a loaf, an entire loaf of warm bread to go with it. His mouth was watering by the time they were home. And he could smell the bread baking as soon as he got out of his car.

After dinner, he heard from Chalina again. They'd be arriving tomorrow at the Columbus airport. He told her that he'd be there to get her as it was Wednesday because he and his wife had some shopping to do. Then he told her about the decorating contest. He, too, was surprised at how easy it was to talk to her and wondered if one of his brothers was getting a mate. Then, he dismissed that idea. It usually didn't work that way, he didn't think.

That night, when he finished up with the program sheets that he'd gotten in the mail, Loren couldn't believe how generous the colleges were being to the kids here. Of course, they all had heard about what had happened. It had been worldwide news for about a week after it all happened. Even the funerals had been covered by news crews.

Mabel and Clarence were still awaiting arrangements to be made. Since they had children, as it turned out, only the one, they had decided to wait for them to make them. The funeral home that had their bodies had said that they were getting a lot of arrangements for Clarence specifically and none for Mabel at all.

Teddy and Mike's funeral had been held at the high school. Both of them had so many arrangements that they didn't fit in the large gym. After filling up the room with as many as they could get in there with the people they had expected to come, the florists started lining the parking lot with them. And they were coming from all over the world too.

Once the funeral was over, the florist were able to break down most of the arrangements and send them to the nursing homes. With the families permission, of course. Mike's wife had asked, too, that donations be made to the football team in honor of her husband. Thousands of dollars had been donated to the cause, and it looked as if they were going to be able to not only get new uniforms but some much-needed equipment as well.

The football stadium was going to be renamed, too. It was going to be called the Micheal and Theodore Stadium in honor of the fallen. It still brought tears to his eyes when he remembered the look on Sarah's face when the unveiling was done just days after the funerals.

"I got a call from my dad today." He asked her if she was all right. "I am. He's wanting me to give him magic again, of course, but he also asked me if I could give him some money. He's been kicked out of the shelter twice now for complaining about his ailments. He's lucky that I'm not in charge of the place, or I wouldn't have allowed him to be there at all."

"You're a good daughter." When she smacked him, he laughed. "All right. We're going to have company tomorrow. The little girl is Lynnett, but she goes by Lynn. She's nine years old and, from what I have been able to find out, a good kid. It's been harder to get much on Chalina. She works from home for some insurance companies and has money in the bank. Also, we'll need to keep an eye out for her ex-husband. He has a heavy fist when it comes to Chalina. I have a feeling, though, that Lynn has no idea that her dad abuses her mother still. I think also that Chalina doesn't talk bad about Chad, but she could."

"She didn't admit that he broke her ankle, did she?" Loren said it didn't appear so. "We'll keep her safe. The little girl, too."

When they went to bed that night, he was actually looking forward to the next day. It had been a while since he'd been happy to get out and about. He was going to have to thank Jeremiah for telling him about the job. He might even take him out to dinner for it.

Smiling, Loren thought that he couldn't have been happier right now. He could only hope that when the others got their mates, they were even half as happy as he was. They'd be on top of the world right there with him.

AWARD WINNING, BESTSELLING AUTHOR

Kathi Barton, a winner of the Pinnacle Book Achievement Award and a best-selling author on Amazon and All Romance books, lives in Nashport, Ohio, with her husband, Paul. When not creating new worlds and romance, Kathi and her husband enjoy camping and going to auctions. She can also be seen at county fairs with her husband, an artist and potter.

Her muse, a cross between Jimmy Stewart and Hugh Jackman, brings her stories to life for her readers in a way that has them coming back time and again for more. Her favorite genre is paranormal romance, with a great deal of spice. You can visit Kathi online and drop her an email if you'd like. She loves hearing from her fans. aaronskiss@gmail.com.

Follow Kathi on her blog: http://kathisbartonauthor.blogspot.com/

www.ingramcontent.com/pod-product-compliance
Lightning Source LLC
Chambersburg PA
CBHW030226180626
46810CB00008B/2988